THE DOGLEG
MURDERS

CHRISTOPHER BRYAN

Diamond Press

The Dogleg Murders

Christopher Bryan

Printed in the Unites States of America

The Diamond Press

Proctors Hall Road

Sewanee, Tennessee

For more information about this book or the author, visit
www.christopherbryanonline.com

Edition ISBNs

Trade paperback: 978-0-9853911-9-5

e-book: 978-0-9978496-0-8

Library of Congress Cataloging-in-Publication data is available upon request.

First Edition 2016

Cover design by Kara Kosaka

Book design by Christopher Fisher

Diamond Press logo by Richard Posan for 2 Ps

Photograph of Christopher Bryan by Wendy Bryan

.

In memoriam
Leslie Stemp
1894-1968
John Hull
1931-2015

But the souls of the righteous are in the hand of God,
and there shall no torment touch them.
(Wisdom 3.1)

THE DOGLEG MURDERS

PROLOGUE

Thursday, 1ˢᵗ September 1994,
Abbott's Lane, Alphington, near Exeter, in the county of Devon.
Near to the golf course of the Alphington Golf and Country Club.
About one o'clock in the afternoon.

What on earth was the boy staring at?

He stood motionless, battered school exercise book in one hand, his royal blue school cap and blazer vivid against the dark green hedgerow behind him.

Ah — *that's* what he was looking at!

About fifty meters to his left a group of girls in shorts and tee shirts had turned onto the lane. They were pretty girls and at thirteen years already he was feeling the mystery and enchantment of the opposite sex.

So he stood fascinated. Indeed so fascinated, so transported with the view and lost, he quite failed to notice a footfall on the grass behind him, or the golf iron that hung poised for an instant above him, silhouetted against blue sky and sun, and then descended hard onto the back of his head.

For the tiniest fraction of a second he was aware of the crack against his skull and what seemed like a flash of blinding light —

Then, blackness.

The girls, occupied as they were with their own conversation and laughter, were hardly to be blamed if they noticed nothing when they arrived at the spot where the boy had been standing. The dents in the turf and the broken grass where his feet scraped along the ground as he was dragged into the bushes were, after all, very slight.

And beyond that, from the lane at least, there was nothing else to notice.

ONE

Monday, 26 October 2015 — just over twenty-one years later.
The Blossoms Residential Home for the Elderly,
Crawford Road, Exeter.

"Father Michael! Do you have a minute?"

It was Mrs. Lofton, the matron.

Michael Aarons, rector of St. Mary's Church, Exeter, turned and waited as she came down the stairs.

Some retirement homes smelt like urinals. They were really depressing. Some smelt of disinfectant and carbolic, which was better, but still left you wondering what *other* smells were buried beneath the carbolic.

And some — the nicest kind — smelt like ordinary homes. The Blossoms, happily, was one of them: a pleasant old house set in splendid gardens. In its previous life it had been a boys' prep school. The staff was well trained, cheerful and caring. And Mrs. Lofton, buxom and bouncy, seemed just the right person to be in charge of it.

"Father," she said quietly when she was by his side, "there's a new lady on the second floor in number three. Jenny Farthing. She has emphysema, and I don't think she's got long. She's very nice, always a little joke and a smile for everyone, but to tell you the truth, Father, I think she's sad. And she's a bit lonely.

I mean, she doesn't seem to have anyone, no family or anything to come and see her from outside. I bet she'd really like a visit from you, if you had time. Shall I show you? Have you got time?"

Michael had finished visiting his own shut-in parishioners, and was now preparing to go home and write the parish letter, which he would just have time to do before he went to see the ladies of the parish, who were about to make their annual cheese balls.

Cheese balls, as he had discovered soon after his arrival in the parish of St. Mary's, were an important part of Christian life — their importance long predating his arrival. Each year, during the days leading up to Advent, the ladies of the parish made handsome cheese balls that were perfect for hors d'oeuvres — an idea, he gathered, that someone had brought to them some years ago from America. The cheese balls were then sold for five pounds apiece, and since the ladies between them generally made about nine hundred of the things, this meant a handsome sum to go to the parish's overseas mission giving.

A critical stage in this annual enterprise was, however, that it began with four of the ladies each making a different kind of cheese ball to a recipe of her own choice. It was then the rector's job, after a solemn blind tasting, to select the one he liked best. Whichever he chose became that year's recipe for "the rector's cheese balls." All this, when explained to him, had seemed perfectly reasonable. Except that when he told his wife Cecilia about how the parish ladies would be selling "the rector's balls" to support overseas mission, she had dissolved into paroxysms of gleeful laughter. It all came, he thought, of his having married an Italian police officer instead of a nice, staid, English lady who would have understood about cheese balls.

Be that as it may, tasting cheese balls is what he was supposed to be doing after he'd written the parish letter. Except that if he stayed here at The Blossoms and visited Jenny Farthing, there wouldn't be time to write the parish letter, because he certainly couldn't postpone the tasting of the cheese balls. Some things are not negotiable. And that in turn would raise the question, when *would* he write the parish letter, which was supposed to be posted on the parish website tomorrow morning, first thing?

"Of course I've got time," he said.

Two

In front of a house in a street off Burnthouse Lane, Exeter.
The same day, and about the same time.

Detective Inspector Verity Jones of Exeter CID looked up at the front of the house just in time to notice the half brick that had been tossed from a third floor window and was now flying in a graceful parabola toward the head of her friend and superior officer, Detective Superintendent Cecilia Anna Maria Cavaliere, also of Exeter CID.

There really wasn't time to talk about it.

She hurled herself at Cecilia, taking them both down onto unkempt grass and weeds alongside the path.

"Verity!" Cecilia said, flat on her back among dandelions and dead leaves. "I'm flattered of course, but isn't this very sudden? Especially with you being a married woman and all?"

"Ma'am," Verity said — and pointed to where the half brick had landed with a brutal thud. It had cracked the paving stone on which Cecilia had just been standing.

"Oh," Cecilia said.

She sat up, brushing away leaves and grass, and blinked at the half brick.

"Verity Jones," she said after a moment of further consideration, "I think you just saved my life. Thank you."

"Don't mention it," Verity said.

A gruff voice, strongly Devonian, came from their right and somewhat above them —

"Shall we go in, then?" It was Sergeant Stillwell, uniformed, over six-feet tall and broad in proportion, gazing down at them. Whenever he was free at weekends he played rugby for the Exeter Saracens. He was gesturing toward the front door.

"We'd better get the silly little bugger, hadn't we, ma'am? He's obviously a bloody maniac."

"Good idea, Sergeant," Cecilia said. "Go for it!"

Bill Stillwell needed no second invitation. His kick toward the Yale lock was perfectly placed, and the front door burst inward. He was not a rugby player for nothing.

He entered the house, followed by two constables.

Donald Jackson, petty thief and wannabe tough guy, was still leaning out of the third story window from which he had thrown the brick, happily engrossed in jeering down at the two women police officers he'd just spotted getting to their feet and dusting each other down. They were in plain clothes but even without the two police cars parked in the road he reckoned he'd have known what they were a mile off. He had an instinct for these things.

"Are you two *it*?" he yelled. "Is that *all*? Christ, my old grand-mother could have seen you two off! Hadn't they got anything better to send? Haven't you lot *got* any *real* coppers any more? I want to see some *proper* filth!"

At which moment there was a rattle and a bang from behind him. He turned as the door burst open to reveal the burly, uni-formed figures of a police sergeant and two constables.

"Now then, my lad," the sergeant said, striding into the room, "what's all this about you wanting to see some *real* coppers?"

"Oh shit," Jackson said.

THREE

The Blossoms Residential Home for the Elderly.
A few minutes later.

It was a large, pleasant room with cheerful green and yellow wallpaper and curtains to match, and a big window looking out onto birdfeeders and trees and sunshine beyond them. Mrs. Lofton and Michael found Jenny Farthing sitting up in bed: a tiny person in a blue bedjacket with white hair in a neat page-boy cut, oxygen equipment by her side and an oxygen mask to hand. She was watching the birds as they clustered and fluttered around the feeders.

She smiled and did indeed seem pleased to see him.

"Though I'm not really one of yours," she said to Michael in what he thought was an East London accent. "We was Methodist when I was little, though I haven't been for years."

"Would you like me to ask the Methodist minister to come and see you, Mrs. Farthing? He's a good friend of mine."

"'Jenny' will be fine, Father. No, you'll do. Fact is I've always had a soft spot for C of E, especially when it's high. Some people don't like it; say it's too posh and formal. But me, when it comes to the Almighty, I'm all for a bit of bowing and scraping!"

Michael nodded, and conceded that in matters involving the Almighty he too was inclined to a bit of bowing and scraping.

After Mrs. Lofton had left them he perched himself on a chair by the window and they chatted. They chatted first about birds, a subject on which Jenny Farthing was clearly knowledgeable. She pointed out to him the different kinds that they were seeing: mostly blackcaps and chiffchaffs.

"But you never know what'll turn up if you watch long enough! You just have to be patient. And not be disappointed if you don't see nothing special for a bit! And then just when you're not expecting it something wonderful turns up. There was a short-eared owl the other day. Lord only knows what he was doing here on our windowsill at three in the afternoon!"

Perhaps it was really an angel disguised as an owl.

"That's amazing, Jenny."

"'Course sometimes there's no one at all—like one day last week. They'd all decided to go somewhere else for their dinner! Lots of lovely nuts in the feeders and not a blooming one of them turned up!"

After a while she began to tell him something about herself.

She was indeed, as he suspected, a Londoner: from Stepney to be exact—"I'm a cockney sparrow," she said proudly. But then she'd fallen for a young man who was a keeper of the grounds at Kensington Gardens, and married him. And after a while he'd been offered a job as groundskeeper at the Alphington golf club in Devon, and as they'd both dreamed of living in the country one day, they'd moved west to Alphington, and here they'd stayed and been happy.

But Mr. Farthing had passed on by now and Jenny Farthing was a widow and had been for some years.

Michael sensed as she told him this last that there was more to say—that all here was not well. And Mrs. Lofton had said she thought Jenny Farthing was sad. But for the moment he held his peace.

There were photographs on the bedside table. He pointed to

one of a very pretty girl, ash blonde with a pageboy haircut like Jenny's.

"What a beautiful girl!" he said.

"That was me!" she said, perking up. "I was a bit of all right, wasn't I?"

"You certainly were!"

He had a sudden sense of Jenny Farthing as she must have been when she was young: pert and pretty, funny and cheeky. A cockney sparrow! And surely a bit of all right! But now the years — and, most likely, cigarettes — had done this to her.

There were other photographs. Here was a nice looking man in his mid-thirties — presumably her deceased husband? Maybe it was best to leave that for the moment. Here was a boy in his teens, smiling self-consciously at the camera. The face was sensitive, gentle, and intelligent, with something in it of the older man — who must, surely, be his father? It was a beautiful photograph, and he could quite see why Mrs. Farthing would like to have it near her.

"That's a nice photograph," he said, which seemed a harmless enough remark.

At which Jenny Farthing burst into tears.

FOUR

The garden of the same house in a street off Burnthouse Lane.
A few minutes later.

Now under arrest and handcuffed, it was undoubtedly a more subdued Donald Jackson who appeared in what was left of the front door, escorted by the Sergeant Stillwell and the constables. Yet still he was not so subdued as to be beyond eyeing up Cecilia and Verity.

"Jeez," he said, "close up you two ain't half bad!" Having perhaps a preference for petite blondes, he focused his charms on Verity. "So what you doing tonight, eh, sweetheart?"

Verity returned his gaze calmly. "Whatever it is," she said, "it won't be with you."

"Now then, none of that," Sergeant Stillwell intervened, propelling Jackson gently but firmly forward along the path and toward the patrol cars. "*You* just said the superintendent and the inspector weren't good enough, didn't you? *You* wanted to talk to the proper filth. Well that's us, my lad!"

After a few minutes Verity followed them. Normally a model of sartorial perfection, at this moment, thanks to her adventures in the grass, she actually appeared somewhat disheveled.

Cecilia gazed after her for a moment before turning her

attention back to the broken paving stone, the half brick, and the wrecked front door. She stared at them for several minutes.

Finally she gave a little sigh.

"Well," she said quietly and to no one in particular, "I dare say that could have gone more smoothly."

FIVE

The supper things had been cleared away — salmon in white wine prepared by Michael: a recipe memorable to him and to Cecilia as the first he had ever cooked for her, long before either of them thought that one day they would be married.

Rachel Rosina Maria their five-year-old and Rosina Anna Maria aged one had been put to bed.

Figaro the dog, faithful guardian, had revolved three times in his own bed on the floor between Rachel and Rosina, and then settled himself down for the evening with a contented grunt. He would no doubt appear in the sitting room at about ten o'clock and expect to be taken for a walk. Felix and Martine the cats had eaten a little supper, allowed themselves to be stroked and adored for several minutes while looking wise and inscrutable, and then disappeared on some business of the night. Water bowls for various creatures had been checked, kitchen surfaces wiped, and Cecilia's houseplants watered. The dishwasher had been loaded and switched on, and was now emitting such squishes and gurgles as indicated it was about its lawful occasions.

Throughout this pleasant exercise in domesticity Cecilia had first recounted in fits and starts the story of her own day, including the flying brick and how Verity had saved her life, and then listened in fits and starts to her husband's adventures. As St. Mark was said to have done of our Lord in the gospel, he told his story "accurately but not in order" — which in this case meant that he started with the cheese balls. Cecilia managed — she was pretty sure she managed — to prevent her lips from curving into anything save the faintest trace of a smile as she listened to this.

"Do you actually *like* cheese balls?" she asked when it was over.

"Lots of people love them," he said.

"That wasn't the question."

"I'm not crazy about them. I mean, I like lots of kinds of cheese. You know I do. Cheddar and Cambozola and Jarlsberg for instance! But I don't really like cheese mixed up."

"Isn't Cambozola a mixed-up cheese?"

"Is it? Well, I like that one."

"So why don't you get someone else to taste the cheese balls? Lots of people love them. You just said so."

"I can't. It's got to be me. It's part of my apostolic duty. I dare say there's something about it in the Bible if I knew where."

"How about 'Eat what is set before you'?"

"Oh I *say*! *Yes*! That really is rather clever of you!"

"Thank you! Though it might be tactful not to sound *quite* so surprised about it."

Finally, as having saved the most important until last, he told her the tale of Jenny Farthing.

It took some time, and when he'd finished, she pursed her lips and sat silent for a moment.

"Right," she said finally, and leaned forward. "Now let me see if I've got this straight. Jennifer Farthing's husband Tom was senior groundskeeper at the Alphington Golf and Country Club. Their son, James, aged seventeen, was a promising young golfer, who would quite probably have made it as a professional. What was it he did when he was fourteen?"

"She says he played off scratch," Michael said. "Which I gather means he was pretty good."

"I dare say it does. Anyway, so far all was well. But then on the morning of the second of September 1994 the body of a thirteen-year-old boy was found near to the course. He'd been beaten to death with a golf club, and then dragged to a ditch and thrown into it. And young James was suspected of killing him. Right?"

"Yes."

"And the reason they suspected him was — what?"

"I'm not sure," Michael said. "Jenny Farthing wasn't very coherent about that. She just kept saying it was all nonsense — as I suppose you'd expect her to. But she says the police brought him in for questioning. So obviously they had *some* reason to suspect him."

"But then they didn't charge him?"

"No."

"So also obviously the reason wasn't very convincing, even to them. But then after they'd released him, he went out and hanged himself? From a tree on the golf course?"

"Yes. Near where they found the body. The tenth hole."

She shook her head. "That sounds to me awfully like an admission of guilt."

"Apparently that's what everyone thought. The police inquiry ended almost at once, and the case was treated as closed. That's what Jenny Farthing tells me. And then to cap it all her husband Tom seemed to lose all his will to live and went to pieces. He died a year later." Michael paused.

Cecilia waited.

"Maybe it's just desperate loyalty," he said at last, "but Jenny Farthing says she's sure the police were wrong to give up the case. She doesn't know why her boy killed himself. She doesn't think it was at all like him to do that. He wasn't a quitter. And in any case she's dead certain he was *not* admitting guilt, because he wasn't guilty. He'd never have hurt anyone. The best she can guess is that he was just terrified and that drove him out of his wits. What she *is* certain of is that his name was blackened and he was driven to his death and her and her husband's lives were ruined for someone else's crime. She's sure of it."

"Which does not, of course, make it so," Cecilia said.

He nodded. "I know. It's just, well, she hasn't got long to live, and she really seems to have no one. She says she just wishes *someone* would take another look at the case. And she's a nice woman. She likes birds, and knows a lot about them. So I thought I'd tell you." He paused, and sighed. "She was stunningly pretty when she was young. There was a photograph of her on the bedside table. Ash blonde with a pageboy haircut! An absolute knockout!"

His wife gazed at him speculatively.

"Could it be," she said finally, "that my highly susceptible husband has fallen in love with a girl in an old photograph?"

He gave a half smile and shook his head. "I don't know," he said. "Maybe."

"All right," she said, "I tell you what I'll do. I'll get them to dig out the file, and I'll take a look at it. If I think there's anything wrong I'll show it to the chief super and see what he thinks. We can surely break that much of a lance for this once-beautiful lady of yours. Heaven knows what we can expect to learn after twenty-ish years, but it can do no harm to look."

"That would be wonderful."

"Maybe it would—but don't get your hopes up! Or hers!" She looked at the clock. "I think I'll go and check on Rachel and Rosina," she said. "Then do you want to watch *The Great British Bake-Off* on I-Player?"

"Absolutely," he said.

SIX

Tuesday morning, 27th October.
Heavitree Police Station. Cecilia Cavaliere's office.

As soon as she arrived at her office on the following morning, Cecilia sent for the files on the 1994 Alphington Golf and Country Club deaths. They arrived about half an hour later, and she spent the next thirty minutes or so examining them—an experience that was, to say the least, depressing.

There were photographs of the two boys as they had been in life. Frank Kermode, the thirteen year old, bright-eyed and cheery, peering at the camera as if he were interested in everyone and curious about all things. And James Farthing the teenager—there was a face to catch her heart! Gentle and sensitive—but there was strength there, too, and good humor.

Both had died too soon. And both, so far as she could see, had died for nothing.

What if they had lived? What discoveries might Frank Kermode's bright curiosity have led to? And perhaps James Farthing really would have become a great sportsman?

No one would ever know.

Thou'lt come no more,
Never, never, never, never, never.

She and Papa used often to read Shakespeare together when

she was a girl, but they'd only read *King Lear* once, or rather tried to read it. Papa had choked and started to weep when he read those lines. Then he'd hugged her and said they'd read no more that day and she, stupid teenager that she'd been, had wondered what on earth was the matter with him.

Back to the file!

What then of the police investigation? It had been led by an officer called — Barnwell, was it?

She checked.

That was right. Barnwell. Detective Superintendent Timothy Barnwell, Exeter CID.

Same rank as her. Same job.

She bit her lip as she read the report.

Much of the work had been meticulous. So far as she could see, DSI Barnwell and his colleagues had interviewed just about everyone in or around the club who could possibly have been a suspect, and they appeared to have checked everywhere they could possibly have checked for the murder weapon. There was certainly nothing to complain of there — except, perhaps, that nothing useful had come out of any of it.

All right.

What then of James Farthing, the suspect, the son of Michael's once-beautiful lady? *Why* was he a suspect?

According to the notes before her, Barnwell had four reasons for questioning Farthing.

First, he had no alibi — he said he'd been at home alone all afternoon, which meant there was no one to bear that out.

Second, Kermode was beaten to death with a golf club, and James Farthing was a golfer. To be exact, the forensic examiner said it looked as if Kermode had been knocked over the back of the head with the golf club first, then beaten to death with it afterwards — "savagely beaten," according to the words of the report — while he was unconscious.

Third, there was blood spattered on the front of Kermode's

clothes, and it wasn't Kermode's. Kermode was B Rhd positive and this was O Rhd positive. What was more, forensics reckoned from the spatter pattern that the bloodstains had resulted from a nosebleed experienced by someone *dragging* the body. It had turned out that James Farthing *was* O Rhd positive, so he could have been that someone.

Fourth, James Farthing had received a warning from a local magistrate six months earlier for flashing.

At which Cecilia raised an eyebrow, and sighed.

She looked through the file again, checking a couple of points, and then looked though her own notes.

She sat for several more minutes, the fingers of her right hand tapping softly on the desk.

Finally, she reached for the telephone.

SEVEN

Heavitree Police Station about an hour later.
The office of the Chief Superintendent.

Chief Superintendent Glyn Davies finished reading about the 1994 deaths and looked up at Cecilia, who was seated opposite his desk. She and Verity Jones, to whom she had also shown the report, were in his office at Cecilia's request.

"So what exactly are you proposing to do with these venerable historical documents?" he said.

"Well sir, I didn't think at this stage I'd involve the team."

The Serious Crimes Team, to which she was referring, had been created in October of the previous year following her return to duty after the birth of her and Michael's second daughter, Rosina. She and Verity Jones had both been promoted at the time, she to detective superintendent and Verity to detective inspector. They now headed a group that also included Detective Constables Tom Wilkins and Headley Jarman, and their brilliant civilian computer specialist, Joseph Stirrup, Verity's Bahamian husband. Verity and Joseph had been married since January of the previous year, and in December had produced a small person of their own, Samuel Michael Immanuel, brown and beautiful, generally referred to by all as "the infant Samuel."

It had already occurred to Cecilia and Verity that it would be very convenient if the infant Samuel and Rosina were to marry each other, although they agreed that it was a little early to formulate wedding plans.

"Apart from anything else," Cecilia pointed out, "the infant Samuel may turn out to be one of those men who fall in love with older women, in which case of course Rachel would be the obvious candidate."

"Very true," Verity said. "We mustn't forget that."

"For the moment," Cecilia said to the chief superintendent, "the team needs to finish up the brewery business" — she was referring to a fairly major fraud involving a local brewery that they had uncovered over the past few months — "but I am sure that you" — she turned to Verity — "and the others can manage that perfectly well without me. Otherwise things seem generally quiet, and if it stays like that, then there are a couple of things in the Alphington file that I *would* like to look into, old though it is."

"And they are?"

Cecilia pursed her lips. "Well, the first thing to say is that Barnwell actually had nothing on Farthing. And never had."

Verity nodded vigorously.

"Taking Barnwell's alleged points in order," Cecilia continued, "one, Farthing didn't have to prove he wasn't at the scene of the crime, DSI Barnwell had to produce some evidence that he was. Two, even if the killer was a golfer, why did that necessarily point to Farthing? The body was next to a golf course, for God's sake! As for three, the blood group, O Rhd positive was — and is — the commonest blood group in the United Kingdom. Establishing that whoever dragged the body was O Rhd positive meant no more than that Barnwell had succeeded in narrowing his possible suspects down to about thirty million people. That's assuming, of course, that you rule out anyone from overseas!"

Verity, who had blown out her cheeks in scorn at the first mention of Farthing's blood group as grounds for suspecting him, again nodded vigorously.

The chief superintendent smiled. "All right, I agree. There was no case. Which was no doubt why Barnwell released him without charge. So what are the things you'd like to look into? And why?"

"First I'd like to know what the flashing was about. I can see why that being on Farthing's record made him a suspect, but since the magistrate let him off with a warning, it can't have been *too* serious. It might have been just a schoolboy dare. I'd like at least to know what his mother thinks happened. It could tell us something about the boy. What he was made of."

Davies nodded. "All right. And what else? You said there were a couple of things."

"The blood," Verity said, clearly unable to contain herself any longer. "Surely someone should look again at the blood?"

Cecilia nodded. "Exactly. We've still got the boy's blood-stained clothes in evidence—I checked this morning. But they didn't generally do DNA testing in 1994, and now we do. I'd like to ask James Farthing's mother for a DNA sample. If she co-operates, then that could be the clincher. We can tell whether the bloodstains on Frank Kermode's clothes were from her son or not. If they were, then surely he did it, and Barnwell was right to home in on him, even if more by luck—let's say a good instinct—than by detection."

"On the other hand, " Verity said, "if those bloodstains *weren't* from James Farthing. . ."

"Exactly," Cecilia said.

There was a pause.

"Of course—I realize with its all being over twenty years ago we may be too late," Cecilia said.

"Our Northern Ireland colleagues have started a new inquiry

about Bloody Sunday," Davies observed, "and that was more than *forty* years ago."

"Really? They surely can't hope to get anyone on that now?"

Davies smiled. "Oh," he said, "I think they may. You just watch. As for this golf club business of yours and Michael's — go for it! And keep me informed."

EIGHT

The Blossom Residential Home for the Elderly. That afternoon.

The room was light and sunny, and today Jenny Farthing had on a pink bedjacket.

"Ooh, you're lovely!" she said when Michael came in with Cecilia and introduced her. "So you're Father Michael's missus?"

"That's me," Cecilia said.

"Well I hope he knows how lucky he is."

Cecilia laughed. "He'd better!"

"That's right, love. Don't let them take you for granted. Make sure they remember you're a princess and they're lucky to have you. My Tom was always good like that."

"I will." Cecilia knelt beside the bed. "Mrs. Farthing—"

"Jenny, love."

"Jenny, I need to tell you that I'm not only Father Michael's missus. I'm also a police officer."

"Blimey!"

"Father Michael thinks you'd like us to look again at what happened—with James, all those years ago. Would you like that?"

"Yes, I would."

"Well Jenny, we'd like to try. But we're going to need your

help. I'm going to have to ask you to talk to me about things that happened then — things I'm sure are very upsetting for you. Do you think you can do that?"

Jenny Farthing picked up her oxygen mask and took a sniff.

"I can try," she said.

Cecilia nodded. "All right." She perched herself more comfortably so that she could listen. "The first thing," she said, "is the story about your son flashing. I've read the official version. Now I'd like to hear yours. His."

Jenny's lips tightened, but she stayed calm, and took another breath of oxygen. "It was all lies," she said quietly. "Our Jimmy was taking a walk in that patch of woods that's by the golf course. He thought there was no one around and so he went for a pee in the bushes. Then this little girl appears out of nowhere and starts giggling. Of course he puts himself away at once — he's really embarrassed. But then some lady who's with the little girl appears. He says who he is and apologizes, and she says nothing much, and he goes off and thinks that's the end of it. But then the lady — lying, toffee-nosed bitch — goes and reports him and says he was flashing at her niece. And the next thing we know we've got police at the door."

She took another breath of oxygen.

"You know the rest," she said. "I think even the magistrates thought it was ridiculous, though I dare say they felt they had to do something. So they gave my Jimmy a warning. But if everyone who ever peed in the bushes got hauled up before the beaks, seems to me they'd never have time to deal with anything else."

Cecilia nodded.

"You know," Jenny continued, "it's not as if Jimmy was lonely or frustrated or anything like that. He had a nice little girl friend. Julie Danvers. I think they were starting to get quite steady. And she stuck by him when the trouble started, come round every night she did. And then she was heartbroken, sobbed her little heart out, when—well, you know, when he—he—" She stopped, and used the oxygen mask.

Cecilia nodded and waited for a moment.

"And—is Julie still around?" she said at last.

"No. She joined the army as a medic and got killed in Afghanistan, poor girl, helping a wounded soldier. 2004. They gave her a posthumous Military Cross. She was a good girl."

Cecilia nodded. Some time ago she'd asked an ex-army colleague who'd come home from the second Iraq War, "What was it like?"

"It was like every damned war," he said, "a waste of good men."

And good women too, it seemed.

This was also, of course, the problem with investigating something that happened twenty years ago. Half the people you'd like to talk to were dead.

"Jenny," she said, "do you know anything about DNA?"

"A bit. It's all about our cells and things, isn't it? And means you can find things out that you couldn't find out before?"

"Yes, it does. The thing is, if you'd give us a DNA sample, then if Jimmy was innocent, that would be a huge help to us in proving it. I've got a kit here. It's easy to use, you see, and would only take a minute."

"Of course I will."

After Jenny had given the sample, she suddenly said, "Of course if you wanted, I could actually give you something from Jimmy himself."

"You could?"

"This locket I'm wearing. It's his hair. I cut it off when he was little—when he went for his first haircut. That'd give you his DNA complete, wouldn't it? You can borrow it if you want. I want it back, mind!"

"A lock of his hair! That would be *incredibly* helpful! Thank you! And I promise you'll I'll take the best care I can of it, and see you get it back." Cecilia hesitated. "But Jenny, there is one more thing about all this."

Jenny took another breath of oxygen and met Cecilia's eye. "I know," she said. "Instead of proving he didn't do it you might prove he did. Right?"

"That's right. I simply don't know what I'm going to find."

That, after all, was why they called it an investigation.

Jenny Farthing nodded. "I *know* Jimmy and I *know* he didn't do a murder, so I'm not worried about that. And if you *did* go and prove I was wrong, which you won't, then at least I'd know the truth."

She took another breath of oxygen, then turned and looked at Michael, who had sat attentive but silent throughout this conversation.

"And Father," she said, "doesn't it say in the Bible that if we know the truth, the truth will make us free?"

Michael nodded. "It does. According to Saint John, our Lord said it."

"Well, there you are then." She turned back to Cecilia. "I loved our lad, and I *will* love him, always, whatever he's done. So—I'll be grateful if you can find out anything at all, and I'll be patient while you're trying to find it, and cheerful when you do find it, whatever it is. I promise!"

Cecilia nodded.

> *She sat like patience on a monument,*
> *Smiling at grief. Was not this love indeed?*

Jenny reached out and touched her hand. "Don't look so worried, love."

Cecilia smiled. "Sorry!" she said.

"Remember, dear," Jenny said, "like the man in the picture says, it'll all be all right in the end. So if it's not all right, it can't be the end yet, can it?"

***

Outside as they were walking toward the car, Cecilia looked at Michael and took his hand.

"I tell you what," she said. "That cockney sparrow of yours is one hell of a lady. I'm half in love with her myself!"

NINE

"Send DSI Cavaliere in," Chief Superintendent Davies said to his secretary via the phone on his desk.

Minutes later Cecilia appeared, carrying an envelope.

"The DNA result from the Alphington golf club deaths," she said. "You wanted me to keep you informed."

"I do," he said. "Give me the short version."

"The blood on the boy's clothes is male," she said. "But it *isn't* James Farthing, or anyone related to him. The profile is completely different."

"It's been run through the national data base?"

"That was the first thing we did, sir. No matches."

The chief superintendent sat back in his chair and looked at her. "So," he said, "there really isn't *anything* to connect James Farthing to Frank Kermode's murder at all. In fact, rather the reverse: it now appears there was a man involved in moving Kermode's body who definitely *wasn't* James Farthing. Which changes the whole picture."

"Yes, sir."

He got to his feet. "The first thing, Cecilia, is that someone needs to go and tell Mrs. Farthing about this. She deserves to know, and the sooner the better."

"I'd like to do that, sir, if I may. If it's okay with you I'll go now — and I'll take Michael with me, if he's free."

"Good. I thought you'd want to do that and it's right you should. If it hadn't been for you we still wouldn't know. In the mean time, the brewery business is all wrapped up, isn't it?"

"Yes, sir."

"Then I want this file distributed to the team. Let them take a look at it. I know it was a long time ago, and prior to this I wasn't sure whether we'd be justified spending time on it or not. But this is new evidence. Contrary to what some people seem to think, there are very few statutes of limitations in English law, and there certainly isn't one for murder."

TEN

Cecilia had feared Jenny might have another coughing attack at the news, but she merely took a few breaths from her oxygen mask and had a little cry, while Cecilia held her hand.

"It's all right, love," Jenny said when she'd finished. "It's just that I'm so happy. I *knew* my Jimmy would never do a bad thing like that—but now everyone else knows. Thank you for listening to me. You're a kind lady."

Cecilia mumbled something incoherent.

"Do you think you can catch whoever *did* do it?" Jenny said.

"I don't know," Cecilia said. "After all this time I suppose whoever it was might be dead."

"Well if he isn't dead, I bet you and your mates can get him if anyone can."

Cecilia looked at Michael, who was sitting on the other side of the bed, and back at Jenny Farthing, who was still holding her hand.

"Well, Jenny," she said, "I promise you this. At least we'll have a damned good try."

ELEVEN

Heavitree Police station. Later the same morning,
DSI Cecilia Cavaliere's office.

The team met in Cecilia's office at 11:00 a.m., as soon as she had returned from the residential home. At her request, Verity and Joseph had already been hard at work, and a file of information on the 1994 deaths had already been sent to each team member's computer. Photographs of the Frank Kermode murder scene and of various individuals who'd been involved in the case, including the police officers who originally investigated it, together with a map of the golf course and its environs, were posted on the whiteboard. There were also photographs of James Farthing's suicide scene.

"You two have been busy!" Cecilia said approvingly as they gathered.

She rehearsed the main details.

"Frank Kermode was a thirteen-year-old schoolboy attending Alphington Grammar: the son of local banker John Kermode and his wife, Georgina Kermode. The boy's body was found in a drainage ditch close to the Alphington Golf and Country Club's course—near to the tenth hole—on the second of September 1994 at about 7:30 a.m.: a woman walking her dog, and the dog found it. The call came to us at 7:36. The woman called us on her mobile phone."

"Which in 1994 will have been one of those digital things they used to have with a little aerial on it," Joseph said. "A Nokia 2110 or something like that. A classy design, actually, though the technology was primitive by our standards."

Cecilia smiled. "Forensics," she said, "estimated the boy had been dead for nineteen to twenty hours: therefore killed the day before, on the first of September, some time between noon and 2:00 p.m. He'd been beaten to death with a golf club. Savagely beaten. His body seems to have been dragged to the ditch from the lane, which, as you can see, goes quite near to the golf course at this point." She pointed to the map. "You see how it bends."

"It does," Headley Jarman said. "A right-angle dogleg. It's the most difficult hole on the course."

Cecilia stared at him.

"If you use a driver off the tee," he said, "you can easily end up in the jungle, but if you use an iron, you may not get a shot at the green."

"And I take it neither of those is good?"

"No, ma'am."

"I also take it you play this game?"

"I do."

"Are you a member?"

He grinned. "Of the Alphington club? No ma'am. I belong to the Exeter club. Alphington is a bit pricey for me—and to be honest, a bit snobby. But I've played there as a guest."

Cecilia nodded. "I'll bear that in mind." She turned back to the white board. "Facts about the Kermode family: all a bit depressing, I'm afraid. John Kermode divorced his wife soon after the death of their son and went off with someone called Claris to live in the British Virgin Islands. His wife stayed behind in Alphington. But we won't get anything out of either of them because in the intervening twenty-odd years they've both died—as I'm afraid is going to be true of quite a lot of the people one would like to interview in this case. But there was—and I assume still is—also a younger sister, Joan, though we haven't sorted out where she is at the moment." She looked at Joseph.

He nodded. "I'm working on that."

"Good. Now, you'll have seen from the file what happened next."

She went on to speak of James Farthing's suicide, of the general assumption that it was an admission of guilt, and the ending of the investigation.

"The new factor, of course, is that after DNA comparison, the blood on the boy's clothes turns out *not* to be James Farthing's, whose DNA we've been able to obtain from a lock of hair loaned us by his mother, as well as being able to confirm it from her own DNA given to us by her. We know it was a man's blood, but we don't know whose."

"James Farthing could still have been involved," Headley said. "Whoever dragged the body might have been an accomplice."

Verity shook her head. "Yes he could, but so could anybody else. We have to step back and see that once we've shown that the blood on the boy's clothing *isn't* James Farthing's, then we have no more reason to connect him to the scene than we have to connect anyone else."

"Except that Farthing was the one who committed suicide."

"Which could be for no other reason than that he was a sensitive kid," Verity said, "who'd been publicly put under suspicion of murder, who already had that flashing thing against him, and was probably terrified out of his wits."

Headley nodded. "Okay. Point taken."

There was a pause.

"Of course whoever dragged the body could simply be dead by now," Joseph said.

"That's true. But it would be nice if we could make sure."

Another pause.

"What about the golf club that was used to kill the boy?" Tom Wilkins said. "What happened to that? Do we have it in evidence?"

"It was never found. DSI Barnwell had all the members' golf clubs in the club searched. They were all clean. And no one said they were missing a club."

Tom persisted. "What about Farthing, though? Did he have a set?"

"Not his own. The Farthings weren't wealthy. The club lent him a set."

"And was one missing?"

"No. And all checked. Clean as a whistle."

"Oh." Tom shook his head.

"And going back to Kermode," Headley said, "another question that we don't seem to have asked yet is, who on earth would *want* to kill a thirteen-year-old schoolboy? What's the motive?"

"Forensics saw no evidence of sexual assault, so that's out."

"Barnwell suggested a schoolboy fight between him and Farthing that went bad," Tom said. "But that's pretty well out now, too."

"I'd doubt it anyway," Cecilia said. "I don't think seventeen-year-olds fight much with thirteen-year-olds. Surely if they're ticked off with them they generally either ignore them or are rude to them?"

"Which still leaves me with my question," Headley said. "Why?"

"Either the boy had something his killer wanted," Verity said, "or he knew something his killer didn't want known, or he was doing something his killer wanted stopped."

Silence.

"Which," she added, "I admit doesn't get us much further."

Cecilia looked at Verity, and then shook her head.

"I'm not sure we can go even as far as that," she said. "I mean, I know you're being logical, Verity. But seeing the *way* the Kermode boy was killed—he was unconscious but then someone just hammered the kid—given all that, I'm wondering just how much *rational* motive we can expect." She paused, looking for words, then continued slowly. "My point is, my instinct tells me this was someone crazy with rage—and rage isn't rational. I'm not saying there wasn't provocation—there must have been *something*. Maybe the boy *did* know something his killer didn't want known—but it might not have been anything that would seem to most of us like a rational motive for murder. Am I making sense?"

"You are," Verity said. "In other words, perhaps we should concentrate for the moment on means and opportunity, and only afterwards ask what might have been the motive. And it just might be something that to most of us would seem quite trivial?"

Cecilia nodded. "Exactly. Obviously we're moving in the dark here, but that's my hunch." She paused again. "Anyway, if we're to manage anything useful, what *is* sure is that we need to get on with it. The chief super is all right with us looking into this for a day or two, but after that, given it's such an old case, I rather think he'll need evidence of some progress."

They nodded.

"So—Joseph, it would be good if we can interview any of these officers from the original investigation. People keep telling me Detective Superintendent Barnwell has disappeared. I'd like to know what that means. Is he dead? Lost his marbles? What? And if none of those things has happened, can he be un-disappeared? Also there were two detective constables working with him, a DC Wesson and a DC Smith."

She gazed at what her colleagues had written on the whiteboard, as if taking it in for the first time.

"*Smith and Wesson*? Really? Did someone make a typo?"

Joseph grinned and shrugged. "Not so far as I can see, ma'am. They really were DC Aloysius Smith and DC Charles Wesson!"

Cecilia shook her head. "Well all right then. I'll believe you. But we still need to know where they are, and, more importantly, can we talk to them?"

"I am on to it, oh mighty one."

"Okay, then here's my plan of attack for the rest of us. I'm going to go in straight away for the top brass at the club. The chief super's office has already called them and told them we are reopening the case on the death of Frank Kermode, and we want to meet this afternoon with their membership secretary and any members who are still around who were members in 1994. Headley, since you evidently understand golf speak, you're with me on that."

"Yes, ma'am."

"Meanwhile, Verity, I'd like you and Tom to nose around the lower echelons. See what you can pick up from the village, the local shops and so on. Does anyone remember anything at all? What were the rumors? It's quite a long time ago, but who knows what sticks in people's minds? Of course there'll be a lot of smart-aleck sarcasm from both lots about us getting on to it so late, but we'll just have to put up with that!"

They nodded.

"One other thing—as a general rule when I'm questioning people I try to get information rather than give it. This case may be an exception to that. Since we've already told Farthing's mother there's evidence suggesting her boy didn't murder Frank Kermode, it's hardly a secret. So—use your discretion. But it may be interesting to let the new information out and watch how people react to it."

Again they nodded.

"Good. Then let's get to it!"

TWELVE

The Alphington Golf and Country Club.
The same day, early afternoon.

"Angels and ministers of grace defend us!" Cecilia said as they drove under leaden skies along a wide drive between immaculate lawns toward the main club building, Alphington House, which was neoclassical and magnificent. "This feels as if we're in an episode from *Downton Abbey*. How long's this club been operating?"

"I think it started in 1895, the same year as the Exeter club," Headley said. "But of course Alphington House itself is much older than the club. We moved into our clubhouse in 1929. I think the Alphington lot acquired theirs a few years earlier — 1919 or '20. Right after the first world war."

Cecilia nodded. "Well, I expect to be greeted at the door by Mr. Carson the butler at the very least."

But no one greeted them.

The enormous front door opened at a touch, and they found themselves in a vast hall, opulently carpeted, with impressive staircases facing them at the far end and large doors on either side. But there was nobody to be seen. The only signs of life came from an open doorway some way down on their right.

Through it could be heard a quiet hubbub of conversation and the clink of glasses.

"They ought to be expecting us," Cecilia said. "Let's go and find someone."

They crossed the hall and walked through the wide-open door to find themselves in another large room, at the far end of which was a well-stocked bar, with men drinking and talking. Several looked up at their entrance and within seconds there was something like silence. A tall, distinguished looking man with a grey moustache approached them.

Cecilia produced her warrant card. "Good afternoon, sir. I am —"

But the distinguished looking man interrupted her. "*If* you are able to read, madam, you should have noticed, boldly written in large and handsome letters on the doors through which you have just passed, that this is an area reserved for *male* members of this club. That means, in case you have difficulty following it, that it is *off-limits* to females. And you, young man, should know better than to bring a woman in here."

Cecilia sensed her young companion stiffening and bridling at this reception and, with some difficulty, swallowed a smile. "Well, sir," she said, "if *you* will read what is boldly written in not-so-large but still handsome letters on the warrant card I'm holding, you'll see that I am a police officer — Detective Superintendent Cavaliere of Exeter CID. This is my colleague, Detective Constable Jarman, also of Exeter CID. My chief superintendent's office telephoned this morning and made an appointment for us with a Mr. Gregory Catesby, your membership secretary. So if we could just be escorted somewhere where the presence of a woman won't cause you quite such consternation as it obviously does here, and if at the same time the membership secretary could put in an appearance, I dare say we shall do very well, sir."

It would, she reflected, be idle to pretend she didn't notice several younger men in the room grinning at this exchange, or that she didn't rather enjoy it.

"Good God! *You* are Detective Superintendent Cavaliere?" he said.

"I am, sir."

He was evidently speechless.

A ginger-headed fellow drinking at the bar intervened. "I'll show Detective Superintendent Cavaliere to the committee room for you, John," he said. "George, go and find Greg Catesby for us will you? There's a good fellow!"

"I don't know about *find*," came from one of the tables, "but at least I can go and *look*."

A young man got up and departed, presumably in search of Greg Catesby.

"I'm Dennis Reeves, the captain," their redheaded guide said as soon as they had left the bar. "Please forgive our president, John Pinkerton! He wasn't overjoyed at the news of police coming here at all, but I dare say he just can't get his head round being hauled over the coals by a *woman*. He's not such a bad chap when you get to know him, but a stickler for the old ways — which if you ask me are doomed anyway and no great loss. Still, they won't die easily while John Pinkerton's around, that's for sure."

Cecilia smiled. "I've had worse receptions, I assure you. We went to question a man the other day and he threw half a brick at me."

"Good Lord! Were you hurt?"

Cecilia laughed. "Thanks to a quick-witted friend, only my dignity!"

They were by now in another large room, down the middle of which was a long and splendid table of polished mahogany, with matching mahogany chairs on either side.

After a few minutes the membership secretary bustled in, a plump, jolly-looking fellow in his late thirties.

"Superintendent," he said, "Constable, welcome to the Alphington Golf and Country Club! I'm Gregory Catesby, membership secretary and treasurer and all that. I'm so sorry I wasn't there to meet you. Tied up with a stupid telephone call, I'm afraid. The boiler system causing trouble and nobody seems to want to fix it for love or money! But now — please, how can I help you? I understand you're re-opening the investigation into the death of that poor lad in 1994."

"That's right," Cecilia said. "We are. Were you here then?"

"Actually I was. Of course I wasn't a member — I was only seventeen, still at Eton. But yes, I was around. It was the summer holidays. My father was club captain. He was a brilliant golfer — everyone said he could have been a pro. Anyway, I remember all the police and reporters, and everyone talking about the boy's death. Awful business. But then — I thought it was all solved at the time with that other poor lad's suicide?"

"So it was generally thought — at the time."

"May I ask why it's being reopened now?" he asked.

"Technically it was never closed, since no one was ever convicted or even charged. But I believe you are getting those of you who were here in 1994 together for us? So why don't I tell you all what's happened when we've gathered, and save you having to listen to the same story twice?"

"Of course, Superintendent. Mind you, after twenty-one years, quite a number of us are no longer around, I'm afraid. My own father and mother were killed in a car accident less than a year after the Kermode murder. While I was still at school."

"I'm sorry to hear it," Cecilia said.

He shook his head. "It was pretty devastating, I'm afraid." He gave a rather sad little smile. "But then, I suppose life has to go on."

THIRTEEN

The back yard of the Cross Keys Pub, Alphington.
About the same time that afternoon.

B ill Walsh, who'd been moving casks, looked up at Verity
Jones and Tom Wilkins, uttered a broad Devonshire "Ah,"
and wiped his hands carefully on his apron. Quite why he did
that Verity couldn't really see, since the amount of dirt and
grease on his hands and the amount on the apron appeared to
her to be about the same. But still, she told herself, we all have
our little ways.

"Yes, I remember well enough," he said. "A right to-do there
was! Police cars and reporters all over the place for days! I
wasn't working here at the pub then—I was over in the shop."

He nodded in the direction of the small general store across
the road.

"Did you know Frank Kermode personally?" Verity asked.

"Oh yes, poor lad. Funny little chap he was. Nice enough,
mind! Always polite he was, when he come in. He was a dayboy
at the grammar. They had a few boarders too, in those days."

"How was he funny, Mr. Walsh?"

"Well, ma'am, I remember he was always going on about
wanting to be detective. And it wasn't bang-bang shoot-'em-up
cops and robbers kind of detective like you see on television. He

wasn't into guns or anything like that. He was on about collecting evidence. He'd always have an exercise book with him—in fact he'd buy them in the shop—and then he'd be writing down where people's cars were parked and who went where and things like that. Quite a little Sherlock Holmes he was! I suppose if the poor lad had grown up he might have joined the police. He'd have been good at it."

Verity pursed her lips. "What about James Farthing," she asked, "the young man who committed suicide? Did you know him?"

"Yes indeed. Lovely lad he was—and a wonderful golfer! They said he was going to make professional one day, you know, and put Alphington on the map! He used to come into the shop regular to buy packets of mixed nuts. Loved his nuts, he did! You'd think they'd have made him fat, but they didn't. Good brain food they are, nuts. And all that carrying stuff about the golf-course and exercise kept him thin, I suppose."

"Did you talk to him?" Tom asked. "After he'd been interviewed about Kermode's killing? After he'd been a suspect?"

"Only once. He came into the shop for his packet of nuts, pretty much as usual."

"How did he seem?" Verity said.

"He seemed all right with it, so far as I could see. Mostly irritated at being accused at all. And I must say he didn't seem to me to be the type to have murdered anyone. Always had a nice word for everyone, a smile and a joke. Nice little girl friend he had too."

"And who was that?"

They knew from Jenny Farthing about a girl friend called Julie, but what if there'd been another one?

"Julie Danvers her name was. But she got killed in Afghanistan. With the army, she was."

All right, no evidence young James was playing the field.

"She got a medal for it, though," he added. "Posthumous."

Dulce et decorum est pro patria mori: it's sweet and beautiful to die for your country. That's what Quintus Horatius Flaccus thought, anyway. And at least he'd been in the army, so presumably he knew something about it.

"So you didn't think he'd killed the boy?" she said.

"No I didn't, not at the time. But then he went and topped himself, and everyone said that showed he had a guilty conscience. So I suppose he must have done it, and I just didn't see it."

Verity nodded. "Well," she said, "new evidence has come to light that suggests he didn't do it. So it looks as if you were right about him after all."

"I'm glad to hear it. Poor lad. What a crying shame it was! But it's a bit late to be coming up with this now, isn't it?"

Again she nodded. "I'm afraid it is. Thank you for your time, Mr. Walsh. You've been very helpful."

Later, Verity and Tom went across to the village shop.

"Hello, Barbie!" the spotty-faced young man behind the counter said as she entered.

"That's Detective Inspector Barbie to you," she said, producing her warrant card, "Exeter CID. And this is Detective Constable Wilkins. Also from Exeter CID."

"Oh, sorry!"

"You should be. How long have you been working here?"

"Since February."

"How old are you?"

"Twenty-one, ma'am."

So he'd scarcely been born when their crime was committed.

"Does the shop sell school exercise books?"

He shook his head. "I think they used to. But they stopped years ago. No call for them these days. Everyone just puts everything on their iPads."

Verity nodded. "Right."

She glanced at Tom, who indicated by a shake of the head that he had nothing to ask.

She pointed to row of little packets hanging by the counter. "What about the mixed nuts, then?"

"50p a packet, ma'am."

"Then I'll have a packet," she said, putting her fifty-pence piece on the counter.

"It was that fellow Walsh at the Cross Keys going on about mixed nuts that did it," she said to Tom, breaking into her packet as they left the shop a few minutes later, "I got to feeling I could kill for a nice salty cashew!"

FOURTEEN

The Alphington Golf and Country Club.
A little later that afternoon.

There were four besides Gregory Catesby who gathered at the big committee table with Cecilia and Headley at a few minutes after three. There was the man who had first addressed them in the bar, John Pinkerton the president, probably a fit mid-seventies, clearly annoyed by the whole proceeding. There was Dennis Reeves the club captain, fit and active looking, probably in his late fifties. There was a man called George Clayborn, big and red faced, and there was another John, John Belmarsh, small and olive-skinned. Both of these, Cecilia reckoned, were in their sixties or early seventies.

Reeves gestured toward an elderly man in white jacket and black bow tie who was hovering in the doorway, "This is the faithful Glossop, our steward. Do you mind if we ask him to bring us drinks? Keeps the wheels oiled, you know!"

Cecilia smiled and sat back, surveying them, noting that they had all already brought more-or-less filled glasses with them. "Not in the least," she said.

"Can we offer you something, detective superintendent?" Catesby said.

She smiled with all her charm. "Thank you," she said, "but no. On duty, for us, it's generally considered bad form."

The drink du jour appeared to be additional large scotches.

John Pinkerton and Gregory Catesby, she noted, refrained, each nodding his thanks to the steward but also indicating that he needed nothing further. Then, when these preliminaries had been taken care of and the steward disappeared, John Pinkerton, scarcely disguising his irritation, turned to her and said, "And now pray, Detective Superintendent, tell us what all this is about."

"As Mr. Catesby may have told you, sir, we are re-opening our investigation into the death of Frank Kermode."

"But surely," Belmarsh said, "that other boy — the one who used to play — what do you call him?"

"Farthing," Dennis Reeves said, "James Farthing."

"That's right, Farthing. Didn't he confess? Wrapped it all up?"

"He committed suicide, sir," Cecilia said.

"That's right. Well, that was as good as a confession, wasn't it?"

"Only trouble was," Clayburn said, looking bigger and more red-faced than ever, "the bugger escaped justice. Should have gone to the gallows. Best place for him."

"For God's sake, George," Reeves said, "we didn't *have* hanging, not in 1994."

"More's the pity. Abolishing the noose was the biggest mistake this country ever made."

"I have," Cecilia said firmly, "read the report of the original investigation, and the statements made at the time by those of you who were here." She addressed herself directly to Pinkerton. "That does not, I think, include you sir?"

"No, it doesn't," he said. "I joined the club in 1995, when we moved down here from London. So I never met either of those poor boys. But of course I've heard about what happened. And

I'm sitting here at this moment, Superintendent, because I am now president of this club and I should like to know what's going on."

"That's entirely understandable, sir, and if none of the other members has any objection, it's fine by me."

There was a pause, and no one spoke.

Cecilia nodded. "My impression from the original statements," she said to Reeves, "is that you knew young Farthing quite well."

Reeves shook his head. "Who knows how far anyone knows anyone? But I spent quite a lot of time with him, and I liked him. His suicide was heartbreaking. But I think all that is pretty well what I said in my original statement."

"It is, sir, and that's fine." She looked at the others.

"He always seemed respectful enough as far as I remember," Clayburn said, "though, of course, I can't say I really knew him. He was the son of the groundsman, you know."

"My recollection of him is that he was rather pleasant," Belmarsh added. "They let him play in the mornings. And the afternoons too, if there weren't too many members wanting to play."

"We were told," Headley said, "that he played off scratch when he was fourteen."

"That's right. He was good. We all thought he'd turn professional in a year or two."

Cecilia looked at Catesby.

He nodded. "I think everyone felt that the loss of such a promising player was a tragedy, and he was about my age, so I suppose I felt it especially badly. I mean, I'm not saying I really knew him well. I was away at Eton much of the time. But I saw him around in the holidays, and I must admit I liked him very much. So I was stunned when it all happened—I mean, his killing the boy and then his suicide. I still find it hard to take."

Cecilia nodded. All this pretty well agreed with what they

had said in their statements twenty years ago. "If I recall your statements rightly, you didn't come into the club at all on the day of the murder, Mr. Reeves. You, Mr. Clayburn and Mr. Belmarsh, played a round together that morning, then left at lunchtime, and you, Mr. Catesby, played a solitary practice round in the afternoon. But none of you recalled seeing anything of either Kermode or Farthing?"

They all nodded.

"So. You are of course wondering why we have reopened our inquiry into Frank Kermode's death. You may recall from the original investigation that there was blood spattered on the murdered boy's clothes. Forensics established that it wasn't his blood, but it was James Farthing's blood group. Which was naturally reckoned to fit with it's actually being Farthing's blood and so with Farthing being the killer. In forensics' view the spatter pattern was the result of a nosebleed by someone dragging the body."

"So?"

"*So* now we have fresh evidence. To be precise, the 1994 investigation didn't make any use of DNA analysis—at that time it was still a very new technique—and now we have. And from that analysis we've learned that the blood spattered on the boy's clothes was *not* actually James Farthing's, but that of some other man. Which means first, that there's now *no* actual evidence to connect James Farthing to the murder at all. And second, that there now *is* evidence that someone else was involved, another man, and most likely the killer."

She watched them carefully.

"Stuff and nonsense!" Clayburn said. "Farthing killed the boy and as good as admitted it."

"DNA does not lie, sir."

"I say again—nonsense! Everyone knows you can't rely on DNA. It's failed as evidence time after time."

"With the greatest respect, sir," she said, "everyone knows

nothing of the kind. It's quite true there were some mistakes and mistrials early on, but they invariably resulted from people mishandling the evidence. Methods have been tightened quite a lot since then, and I don't believe there's the slightest reason in this case to think there's any error."

Clayburn spluttered.

"Of course," Cecilia continued, "you are welcome to check what I'm saying with my superior, Chief Superintendent Davies, or even with the Chief Constable, if you like. But I don't believe it will change anything."

"So how can we help?" Catesby asked quietly.

"It would be an enormous help if, for purposes of elimination, we could have samples of DNA from each of you who were present at the club—"

The four senior members exploded almost simultaneously.

"*What?*"

"Preposterous!"

"Absolutely not."

"Damned impertinence!"

"Detective Superintendent Cavaliere," the president said icily, "this is an old and honourable club. Among its members are men and women who have served their country with distinction in peace and in war. I absolutely cannot encourage our members to go along with your request, which is pointless and insulting."

The other three nodded.

But then Catesby intervened. "No sir, with respect, it's not," he said quietly. "It's common sense. The more people the police can clear from *any* possibility of being involved in that dreadful affair, the more they can focus on where they need to focus. My family name—the honour of my father, who as a soldier put his life on the line for this country—is more important to me than anything else I can think of. There is nothing I wouldn't do to defend it. Yet I was here in the club at the time of the boy's murder, even though I wasn't then a member. So from the police's point of view I must, technically, be a suspect. It's simple logic. Of course I'll give your people a sample, Superintendent, because that way you'll eliminate me and my family, and that way I clear my name and our honour."

"Thank you," Cecilia said.

"And for the reassurance of my friends here, I believe I'm right in saying that a DNA sample given voluntarily to the police to assist in a particular investigation can't be used for any other purpose?"

"That's correct, sir. We're not permitted to keep it and it must be destroyed as soon as we've used it for this particular inquiry."

"Thank you," Catesby said.

There was a pause.

"Do you have any questions, DC Jarman?" Cecilia said.

"No, ma'am. Not at the moment."

She nodded and got her feet. "Then gentlemen, I thank you for your time. Since it's twenty or so years since those deaths, it may be that some of you have thought of things you wish you'd said in your statements at the time and didn't say. If that's the case, Detective Constable Jarman or I will be happy to hear them. You've only to get in touch with us. As for our request for DNA, you are of course perfectly within your rights to refuse it. My colleagues will be here tomorrow morning at ten o'clock. They'll then take samples from those among you who are willing to cooperate with our inquiry. I bid you good day."

"What really irritates the hell out of me," Headley said when they were back in the car, "is that whenever we challenge a liberal leftie, we're puppet hirelings of the fascist oppressor, but if we venture to question the conservative and established pillars of society, then we're being damned impertinent and insulting."

Cecilia had been sensing her younger colleague's frustration for some time. She chuckled. "It goes with the job, Headley. Get over it."

FIFTEEN

Charteris, a small but handsome Georgian house, once a rectory,
on the outskirts of Alphington. Just after 4:00 p.m.

The indefatigable Joseph had had no difficulty finding the senior magistrate who had been involved in dealing with the flashing complaint against James Farthing, since he still lived locally, just outside the village. On being telephoned, he indicated that he would be happy to receive a visit from the police and that, being semi-retired ("whatever that means," he added), he was at home these days most of the time. Joseph called Cecilia on her mobile to tell her all this just as she and Headley Jarman were leaving the golf club, so she decided to make the visit at once.

The rain with which the afternoon began had ceased, and the sun came out. They found Sir Marcus Snowball sitting on his porch in a cane armchair: a lanky, grey-haired figure in cavalry twills and a battered tweed sports jacket with leather patches on the elbows. He was drinking tea and reading a paperback novel. He had to be in his eighties, but was evidently hale and hearty, and so far as Cecilia could see, sharp as a tack.

"It's good of you to see us, sir," Cecilia said as he rose to meet them.

"Not at all, Detective Superintendent, Detective Constable!

You are both engaged in real work, whereas I am merely amusing myself reading a thriller. I was attracted to it because, as you see" — he showed it to them — "it has on the cover a rather splendid picture of the Royal Courts of Justice being blown up. Alas, the story itself does not so far fulfill the promise of that vision."

He offered them cups of tea, which they accepted.

"And of course a piece of cake, Detective Superintendent! And for you too, Detective Constable! A Victoria sponge, made by my sister Petronella. It is just as good as our mother used to make — and that is a compliment I do not pay lightly, dear though my sister is to me."

Tea and cake! The cake looked delicious and Cecilia accepted, although Headley politely declined.

I do believe the dear boy is worried about his figure, she thought.

"There are those purists," Sir Marcus said as he handed her a plate with a large slice of cake on it, "who would insist we only eat Victoria sponge with raspberry jam, but in my doubtless somewhat dissolute family we've always preferred it in its decadent form, with buttercream as well as jam. And when my sister Petronella is feeling especially dissipated, she has even been known to substitute strawberry jam for raspberry."

"Mmmm," Cecilia said. Headley might keep his figure, but he had no idea what he was missing.

"When your chap called just now about the Farthing case," Sir Marcus continued, "I must admit I had to look up my old notes. Memory for names not what it was, I'm afraid! But as soon as I did — yes, of course I remember it, and what happened to the poor boy afterwards. Terrible business."

He paused and drank some tea.

"In my opinion," he said, "the case itself was damned silly. Technically, when James Farthing peed in the bushes he violated a local statute, and since he admitted it we had no choice but to issue a warning. But I was perfectly sure he'd no intention of exposing himself to anyone and in all other respects the action was totally without merit. For God's sake! If everyone who ever took a quick pee in the bushes had to appear before the magistrates, we'd never have time to deal with anything else."

Which was, Cecilia reflected, more or less exactly what Jenny Farthing had said. "What was your impression of the boy himself?" she asked.

"A rather fine young man, so far as I could see: modest and respectful before the court, but firm. He knew who he was. Indeed, they seemed to be a very pleasant family. All of them came to court to support him, which is generally a good sign. Even his girlfriend was there. She became a local heroine in her own right, you know. Julie Danvers. But that was later. A posthumous Military Medal."

"Farthing's mother told us, sir."

"Ah, yes. Well, good people, all of them."

"So what were your thoughts when you heard about Farthing's being a murder suspect, sir?"

"Frankly, I didn't believe it. I still don't. To be blunt, and no disrespect intended, Superintendent, I thought that your colleagues signed off on that case far too easily. I don't know why that boy took his own life, but I don't believe he ever took anyone else's. What I saw in him was a gentle soul, not a murderer."

"Then you may be interested to know that we now have evidence that confirms your opinion."

She told him of the DNA findings.

He nodded. "I'm not in the least surprised, though I'm appalled to think of the injustice we heaped on that poor family. And I suppose this means that you now have to start looking for the real murderer all over again—after two decades for the trail to grow cold?"

"Yes, sir."

"Do you speak Italian, Detective Superintendent Cavaliere, as your name suggests?"

"I do, sir."

"Well then, I can only say, *sta forte, dottoressa Cavaliere!* 'Truth will come to light; murder cannot be hid long.' And personally, I should have thought twenty years quite long enough."

Cecilia smiled. It was not often that someone other than her father addressed her in Italian and quoted Shakespeare to her in more or less the same breath.

"*Grazie!*" she said. "*Farò il proprio meglio.*"

She would indeed do her best.

SIXTEEN

Heavitree Police Station. Later that afternoon.

"I've found Joan Kermode for you," Joseph said to Verity when she got back to Heavitree after her visit to Alphington with Tom. "She's now in New Zealand. Emigrated in 2000. She works for Wellington Electricity. They own and operate the power distribution network for the Wellington region. I've arranged for us to Skype her at nine o'clock this evening our time, which will be eight o'clock in the morning hers. She's expecting us and says she's willing to tell us what she can remember about her brother's death. So we can do it from home? Okay?"

"Very okay," Verity said. "So aren't you a clever chap!"

Some ten minutes or so after that, Gregory Catesby telephoned from the club, asking for Detective Superintendent Cavaliere. As Cecilia was still out, the switchboard put the call through to Verity.

"Detective Superintendent Cavaliere isn't back yet," she said, "but you can leave a message for her on her phone if you like, or I can take a message for her."

"Well," he said, "it's just to say, would you let her know that we've all had a talk and everyone who was here at the meeting this afternoon has now agreed to give a DNA sample. And also I've phoned round and dug up seven other old members who weren't here this afternoon, and they've all promised to be here tomorrow morning for you. So I actually think that will be everyone who was here then except for those who've died."

"That's terrific, Mr. Catesby," Verity said. "I'll pass that on. You've been most helpful."

He chuckled. "Well, I must admit I find your detective superintendent very persuasive!"

Verity laughed. "Thank you, sir! I'll tell her you said that."

Cecilia got back to Heavitree at about a quarter to five, and Verity gave her the news.

"I think the club secretary fancies you!" she said.

Cecilia brought Chief Superintendent Davies up to date with the afternoon's events.

"Good," he said. "That quite often happens. A group is hostile, but then one public-spirited citizen agrees to cooperate and the others are shamed into it—because of course it looks as if they've got something to hide if they don't."

She nodded. "Well, I just hope something comes of it."

"Cecilia, whatever happens you'll have acquired more information. And that's always good. If there *is* a match, then of course that will be splendid. But if there isn't, as is entirely likely, then you and the team just go back and look again at what you *do* have. Remember, you've *already* proved there was a man involved in Frank Kermode's death who wasn't James Farthing, and you know something about that man which, if you find him, will enable you to identify him. That's much more than the original investigation was able to do. Stick to that! That boy wasn't murdered by Martians or goblins or little green men. He was murdered by a human being, and very likely someone local. That's quite a lot to go on. Stick to what you know, and work from that."

SEVENTEEN

Verity's and Joseph's house. That evening.

Cecilia's mama and papa came to St. Mary's Rectory early in the evening to babysit, so that Cecilia and Michael could go out to supper with Verity and Joseph in their little house on the outskirts of Exeter.

On their arrival they were greeted at the front door by Joseph and Verity, together with Samuel in Verity's arms and, scampering around on the floor in front of them, a little black puppy: a smooth-haired, shiny-eyed, wet-nosed, panting, wriggling, squirming, wobbling, jigging, bouncing, licking, tail-wagging ball of adoration and affection that ran from one of them to the other and back again and then back to Verity and Joseph and then back to them and seemed frustrated only in that she could not be with everyone in the world at once, simultaneously loving everyone.

"This is Hoover," Verity announced, "the newest addition to our family. She'd been abandoned and the RSPCA rescued her and she's about six months old and she thinks everybody and everything in the whole world is totally wonderful."

"Her subtitle," Joseph said, "is 'the wobbling thing'!"

"She's lovely!" Cecilia said, having for the moment become the main target for the puppy's worship. She knelt so that she could better return the favor.

"So aren't you a beautiful girl!" She looked up at Verity. "Is she housetrained yet?"

"The RSPCA seems to have managed that. She asks when she needs to go out. She's also had all her vaccinations and neutering and everything. But Joseph's going to put in a dog flap for her like you have for Figaro."

"She could manage for the moment with a cat flap."

"Not for long. Just look at those feet! They're enormous."

"Maybe she'll be a little dog with big feet," Michael said.

"The RSPCA even gave her a microchip," Joseph said. "So that for better or worse she is absolutely impossible to lose!"

"So you see she's a *bionic* wobbling thing!" Verity said.

"Then," Cecilia said, returning her attention to the puppy, "oh bionic wobbling thing, it seems you are perfect in every conceivable way" — and was rewarded for her words by a fresh bout of wriggling and rapture. "But why," she said, looking up again, "is she called Hoover?"

"Watch her eat and you'll know," Joseph said.

"It's shorter than 'Electrolux' or 'Vacuum Cleaner,'" Verity added. "But you may call her 'Hoove' if you like. She doesn't mind."

"Actually she doesn't seem to mind anything much," Joseph said, "just so long as she's included. But she does prefer things that have food in them."

"Sensible dog," Michael said. "I tend to prefer things that have food in them myself."

Accompanied by the wobbling thing, the next item on the evening's agenda was the settling down of young Samuel. Only after this had been accomplished — with many expressions of praise for his extraordinary beauty, remarkable intelligence, rapid progress in understanding, and other amazing and admirable attributes — only after this did the four grownups (of course accompanied by the wobbling thing) proceed to supper.

Joseph and Verity had prepared two Bahamian specials.

First was a chicken souse: this was chicken cooked with potatoes, onion, celery, garlic, whole allspice, limes, and pepper ("Whatever you do, don't eat the allspice—it's just there to give flavor"). It should, Joseph said apologetically, have been accompanied by johnny cake—much like cornbread, but made with flour instead of cornmeal. But there hadn't been time to make that, so there was just French bread from the local baker.

Cecilia thought the whole thing delicious and said so.

"I must admit we're still a bit nervous cooking for you two," Joseph said. "Everyone in your family is such a marvelous cook."

Cecilia exchanged a smile with Michael, who had said much the same thing the first time he cooked for her—the famous occasion of the salmon in white wine.

"I think," Michael said, "Cecilia's papa would say that you and Verity already have the most important thing a good cook needs: you cook *con amore*."

"I'm all for love, but I'm not entirely clear how it makes us good cooks," Joseph said.

"You must love what you cook," Cecilia said, "and you must love the people you cook for. If that's the way you are, then of course you'll cook with *decoro*, which means you'll take trouble over it, and with *sprezzatura*, which means you won't take what you do too seriously and become a bore about it, even though you *do* take trouble over it. Those are both things you can work at. But then if you do those things, the magic happens: which is that just occasionally your food will have *grazia*—grace! But you can't work at that. It either comes or it doesn't. And tonight it did! So cheers for you!"

For dessert, Verity explained to them, they had what would have been a great Bahamian delicacy, guava duff. Except that she hadn't been able to buy guava in the market that day, so she'd made it with apples instead.

"I *think* it's all right," she said.

Again Cecilia thought it delightful and said so.

"And never worry about not having the exact ingredients as described by somebody in a book," she said. "Mama says true cooking is always *arte povera*: which means cooking with what you've got!"

So far, within the space of a few hours, she'd sampled a perfect (and decadent) Victoria sponge, a delicious Bahamian souse (though with French bread, and that was fine), and delightful sort-of guava duff (that was to say, entirely delightful and sort-of guava). And, of course, she had met Hoover the wobbling thing, who having abruptly run out of energy was now lying in blissful unconsciousness draped over Verity's feet.

It had surely been a day to remember.

At nine o'clock they sat around the large screen in Joseph's study while he brought Joan Kermode on line.

Introductions were made.

"It's good of you to give us your time, Ms. Kermode," Cecilia said.

"I don't know that I can be much use. I was ten years old when Frankie died."

"Please—we know we're asking a lot. We'll be grateful if you'll just be willing to tell us what you can remember. Perhaps we could start with the last time you saw Frankie alive. Could you go from there?"

Ms. Kermode considered.

"It was at breakfast on the day he disappeared. We were all together in the kitchen. Mum, Dad, Frankie, and me. We had cornflakes and scrambled eggs. I remember Frankie and me had two helpings each of scrambled egg—we finished off the pan. Then after breakfast Mum took me into Exeter to get some things for school. It was still the holidays, but school was beginning next week."

"What school was that?"

"The Maynard. In Denmark Road. Nice school it was. I loved

it. Frankie went to Alphington Grammar, but that was for boys only in those days. I think it's changed now."

"So you went off shopping with Mum, and left Frankie. And that was the last time you saw him?"

"Yes."

"Do you remember what Frankie was planning to do?"

"He was going to ride his bike with some of the other boys in the village. I know that because I remember mum telling him not to go beyond the village where it was safe, even if the others did."

"And do you think perhaps he did go beyond the village?"

"No, I don't. But I do think he must have changed his mind about going with the other boys and decided to go detecting instead."

"Detecting?"

"Yes. That's what he called it. He liked to watch what was going on in the village and then write it all down in exercise books that he used to buy at the shop in the village. Where he'd seen people's cars, who went where, that sort of thing. Mum and Dad didn't like it—especially Mum. She called it spying and said it would get him in trouble. She said people don't always like you knowing things about them. But he said one day he was going to be a detective and he was practicing, and that he was very careful and nobody would ever know he was doing it. And nothing Mum or Dad could say ever seemed to stop him."

Cecilia exchanged a glance with Verity. *Why kill a thirteen-year-old? He knew something his killer didn't want known or he was doing something his killer wanted stopped.* Verity merely raised her eyebrows and gave a faint shrug.

Cecilia returned her attention to the screen. "Do you think your parents told the police about this detecting?"

"I know they did. I remember a big, burly man, the chief detective—what was his name? Branley? Barker?"

"Barnwell?"

"Yes, that's right. Barnwell. Well I know mum and dad told him, because I heard them do it. You know, afterwards, when all the police were around."

"That was sensible of them," Cecilia said.

There was a pause. It was ended by Verity.

"Going back to the day Frankie disappeared," she said, "when did you first realize he was missing?"

"We first began to get worried when he didn't come in for his lunch. He was supposed to be back at one thirty. Me and Mum had hurried home specially from shopping so she could get him something. Then when he didn't turn up she phoned round all his friends' parents, and they hadn't seen him. Then she phoned dad at the bank, and finally dad phoned the police."

"So then?"

Joan Kermode hesitated, and shook her head. "I'm sorry — then it all gets a bit blurred. I know we were in an uproar and Mum and Dad were having fits. Mum kept making food that no one wanted to eat and Dad kept taking showers. I went to bed. I think I stayed there for hours. Then finally the next day — Friday — they found Frankie's body and the police came round and told us and it was even more awful. But then after that it's all a bit confused. I'm sorry. I think Mum and Dad had to go and identify the body at some point."

"You've done very well. It was a long time ago."

"I suppose it was. But it did completely change my life, so you'd think I'd remember."

Cecilia heard herself making what Michael called her "mother confessor's encouraging little 'hmm?' noise," and waited.

"Before Frankie died," Joan Kermode said, "we were happy. I was, anyway. I'd had a lovely childhood. I was a Brownie and then a Girl Guide, and Frankie was a Cub and then a Scout, and Mum and Dad were involved and we all used to go to church together and I used to climb trees and it was nice. But then when Frankie died everything fell apart. Dad was out all the hours God gave, working, so he said at first. But soon even I knew he was really with other women. And then Mum got depressed and bitter and angry. And by the time I was fifteen or sixteen I just felt I couldn't ever do anything right for her."

"I'm sorry."

Joan Kermode shrugged. "The fact is, when you realize your family was really all about your big brother and that you didn't actually matter, it isn't the greatest boost in the world for your ego. I was glad to get away finally and go to college. And then while I was in college Mum and Dad both got sick, and died. Within a few months of each other, actually. Dad died in the British Virgins, where he was living with his latest woman, and Mum still in Alphington. And the truth is, by then I hardly felt a thing." She looked away for a moment, and sighed.

You do still feel, Cecilia thought, *and quite a lot.* But she said nothing, since she could think of nothing appropriate to say. She just nodded, slowly.

"I think," Joan Kermode said after a long pause, looking back at the camera, "that that's about all I can tell you. I hope it's helpful. And don't get me wrong. I did love my big brother and we had some good times together. If someone else murdered him, and it wasn't that Farthing boy that everyone thought it was, then whoever it was I hope you get the sod."

"We'll try," Cecilia said gently, "and you've been very, very helpful. Just one last question: you said Frankie used to write down things from his detecting in exercise books. Do you have any idea what happened to those books?"

"Mum gave them to the detective — the man called Barnwell. There were about a dozen of them, I think. Quite a little stack! I remember the detective bundling them up and taking them away."

"And nobody returned them?"

"No. Actually Mum said not to bring them back. She didn't

like them — as I told you. Do the police keep this stuff? Or does it get destroyed?"

"On an unsolved case? We keep everything. Indefinitely."

"Well, then you must still have them."

Cecilia nodded. "Yes, I see. We must." She looked at the others.

"What about the bicycle?" Verity said.

"The bicycle?"

"I think you said that Frankie was planning to ride his bike. What happened to it? Did the police have that too?"

Joan Kermode shook her head. "You know, I honestly haven't the slightest idea. I just don't remember anything about the bike afterwards."

"The police didn't have it?"

"Maybe they did. I don't think it ever came home. But I don't know. I suppose everyone just had other things to think about."

"Do you happen to remember what kind of bike it was?"

"Oh yes, I remember all right! It was a Raleigh — three speed Sturmey-Archer gears, the lot. It had been dad's bike when he was a boy. Frankie was terrifically proud of it. Said they didn't make them like that anymore."

"Do you remember the color?"

"Black, I think. Yes, certainly, black."

"But you don't know what happened to it?"

"Not a clue. Now that I think about it, I wish I did. But I don't."

There was a pause.

Cecilia looked at the others, who shook their heads and indicated in various ways that they had no more questions. She turned back to the screen.

"Well, thank you, Ms. Kermode. I dare say this hasn't been easy for you. We're immensely grateful."

Eighteen

St. Mary's Rectory. Friday, 30th October, 7:55 a.m.

The phone rang on the hall table.

Cecilia was upstairs in the bathroom with Rachel and Rosina. Michael was still in church at the early service. After that he was to catch the train to London for his regular monthly meeting and lunch with his spiritual director, a priest with the Jesuit community in Farm Street. Mama had just arrived with her and Papa's dogs Tocco and Pu to babysit for the day, and was taking off her coat.

The phone continued to ring.

She looked around her for a moment and then, as no one appeared, stopped taking off her coat and answered it.

It was Verity, clearly in something of a panic and wanting to speak to Cecilia.

"I think she'll be a few minutes yet," Mama said. "Can I take a message?"

"Oh, please, would you? The thing is, we're in a mess. I'm so sorry. We feel like complete idiots. But the baby-sitter's just phoned and says she's ill with her sinuses and can't come in today. Joseph's ringing round trying to find a sub, but for the moment, until we do, one of us is stuck. Joseph thinks maybe it ought to be him, since he can do some computer work from home, but we thought Cecilia should decide. I'm supposed to be going at ten with some of the others to collect DNA samples from the Alphington golf club, but we were *all* supposed to start the day in Cecilia's office at eight thirty."

Mama laughed at this tale of woe. "Oh you poor things!" she said. "Why don't you bring Samuel round here? Bring all his bits and bobs and I can look after him for the day if that's all your problem. And what about your new dog?" Of course Michael and Cecilia had told Mama and Papa about the addition to the Stirrup-Jones family when they returned home the previous evening. "You'd better bring her too. You can't leave her alone in the house all day. She'll probably get lonely and chew the furniture!"

"Oh, could you? Would you? That would be marvelous— but—you're already coping with Rachel and Rosina."

"I'm coping with two small people and three dogs, so I dare say I can manage one additional small person and a puppy."

Cecilia came down the stairs, her coat on and obviously ready to go.

"Verity and Joseph have lost their babysitter and are worried about how they can get to work," Mama said. "I told them to bring Samuel and the puppy over to your house. I can manage them as well as Rachel and Rosina. Is that all right?"

Cecilia laughed and hugged her mother. "Oh Mama, you're a brick. Of course it's all right—you're the one who's going to be doing all the work! If *you* don't mind, please, knock yourself out, as the Americans say!"

So the domestic crisis was solved, the infant Samuel and the wobbling thing were duly deposited at the rectory, and the entire Serious Crimes Team met in Cecilia's office on time, as planned.

NINETEEN

Cecilia began by assigning some left over tasks from the brewery business, and then brought Headley and Tom up to date on last night's conversation with Joan Kermode. She suggested they watch the recording of it, in case they saw anything that the others had missed.

"Now," she said, "what about these exercise books the boy was using? According to Joan Kermode her parents handed them over to Barnwell and his colleagues in the original investigation and never took them back. So they should still be in evidence. Yet I didn't notice them at all when I checked earlier. Joseph, could your folk see if they can do a better job of looking for them than I did? We really need to know what's in them."

Joseph nodded. "I'll get them onto it. Frankly, I'm surprised there's no reference to those books in Barnwell's own write up of the case — unless I've missed it?"

The others shook their heads.

"Presumably Barnwell decided the boy's jottings weren't significant enough to consider," Headley said.

"Presumably he did," Cecilia said. "But let's remember what DI Jones said yesterday — that perhaps Frankie knew something his killer didn't want him to know. That 'detecting' of his could have been just what set things off. I think Barnwell was wrong to ignore those books. And I hope your minions can find them."

Joseph nodded. "We'll look for them."

They looked at each other. Cecilia glanced up at the clock.

"It's time for you and your team to be on your way to Alphington," she said to Verity.

"On it, ma'am!"

Perhaps John Pinkerton had come to terms with his surprise over women police officers being in senior positions. Perhaps he preferred neat Welsh blondes to tall raven-haired Italians. Whatever the truth, the fact was that when Detective Inspector Verity Jones, Detective Constable Tom Wilkins, and two uniformed constables arrived at the Alphington Golf and Country Club at the time appointed that morning they were received courteously, took their DNA samples from everyone present who could possibly have been involved in the events of 1994, and departed without incident. They were back in Heavitree well before noon, and the samples were duly dispatched to the lab.

TWENTY

Twenty-four hours later, the results of the DNA sampling arrived from the laboratory.

In one respect Cecilia's worst fears were realized. There was no match to the blood on Kermode's clothes.

There was, however, a match to something else.

"It's him, sir," Cecilia told Glyn Davies. "The 'silent rapist.'"

She was referring to a matter of serial rape in Exeter and the surrounding villages that had been baffling the police for eight frustrating years—since 2007, to be exact. The police had the rapist's DNA, and had had it from his first reported crime. They had a strong suspicion that he was a local man. But they had nothing else—until now.

"Who is it?" Davies asked.

"It's Dennis Reeves, the club captain."

"And there's no possibility of mistake?"

"I don't think so, sir." She paused. "I mean, I find it hard to believe. I *liked* the man. I thought he was drinking too much—but this! I'd never have thought it. But it's his DNA. Not a doubt of it. They got a match. They say they triple-checked it. And of course it's useless."

"I know."

It was as Gregory Catesby had pointed out and Cecilia had confirmed at her original interview with the club members: in the United Kingdom, a DNA sample given voluntarily for the purpose of helping a police inquiry could be used only in the inquiry for which it was collected and must then be destroyed.

So how had it happened that they now knew the rapist's identity? Certainly it wasn't a result of careful detective work. It wasn't even the result of some brilliant though illegal detective instinct. It had come about through sheer dumb luck, probably coupled with laziness. Someone at the lab, instead of isolating the particular sample they were interested in, had simply run the samples they had taken at the golf club through the entire United Kingdom National Criminal Intelligence DNA Database—assuming, reasonably enough, that if none of them matched anything in the entire database, evidently they must not match the one sample they were interested in.

And so it had proved.

Except that Dennis Reeves's DNA did match something. Not the something they were interested in as far as the murder of Frank Kermode was concerned, but something else.

"He *is* the rapist, sir. And there's not a damned thing we can do about it."

The chief superintendent gave a deep sigh and nodded.

"All right, Cecilia. There *is* nothing you can do about it. You're quite right. So keep your team working and continue to focus on the Kermode and Farthing deaths. As for this rapist business, let me think about it."

Glyn Davies downloaded to his computer the file on the so-called "silent rapist," and over lunchtime sat reading it. It did not make pretty reading. He would have preferred not to believe what it told him. Assuming all the rapist's victims had come forward—and of course there might well be some who had not—he had done his work in 2007, 2009, 2011, and 2013. His MO was simple but effective—a young woman attacked from behind, hand over mouth, knife to the throat, and then dragged somewhere—into bushes, behind a wall, behind a building. The rapist never let his victims get a sight of him. He always wore a ski mask and hood, was always gloved, and dressed in black. And he never spoke, so there was no accent or voice to recognize—hence, of course, his nom de guerre, bestowed on him by local media: a nom de guerre, it should be said, that irritated Glyn Davies every time he heard it. "Does the fool imagine rapists usually take time for a little chat?" he'd muttered to Olwen recently when a reporter used the expression on BBC Southwest.

What it all boiled down to, of course, was that their man was good at what he did.

And now they knew who he was.

And as Cecilia Cavaliere had pointed out, they couldn't do a damned thing about it.

Glyn Davies got up and paced the room.

He wanted a cigarette.

He shook his head. He hadn't smoked for twenty years.

It could be his own daughter next—his and Olwen's beautiful Arwen. It could be *anyone's* daughter. And in any case it would be *someone's* daughter: a woman, a citizen, a fellow human being traumatized, her life scarred forever.

He sat down again behind his desk.

So they knew who the rapist was and they really couldn't do a thing about it?

God damn it! That was bloody ridiculous.

Yet it was the way things were. They really couldn't... unless they got a sample of his DNA in some other way.

Some *legal* way.

If, for example, Reeves were *arrested* for any reason, he'd be obliged to give a sample and that sample would automatically go into the national database. And the national database would catch the match.

But then, what possible reason could they have for arresting such a man? Such a respectable and respected citizen, captain of the Alphington golf club, pillar of his community, scion of a fine family?

Davies gave a deep sigh.

He sat still and silent for a long time.

At last he said "Hmmm!" and reached for the phone.

A colleague owed him a favor. He called it in.

Next he called Cecilia. "Cecilia, I'd like to borrow a member of your team tomorrow. To be precise, I'm going to need your golfer, Headley Jarman. It's for a special little op. I think you'd approve, but I'd like to keep the details to myself."

"Of course, sir. Do you need to brief him? Shall I send him along to your office now?"

"That would be good. Thank you."

"Sit down, please," Glyn Davies said when Headley entered his office a few minutes later. "I understand you're a member of the Exeter Golf and Country Club."

"Yes, sir. Our family has been for years."

The chief superintendent nodded. "And I think Exeter club members and Alphington club members share some reciprocal membership privileges. Is that correct?"

"That's right, sir. The restaurants, the bars, and, of course, occasionally playing on each other's courses."

"So if at any time you wanted to have a casual drink in the Alphington bar you'd be entitled to?"

"Yes sir. If I was questioned I'd just have to show I was a member of the Exeter club."

"Good. Now listen, Jarman, here's what I want you to do."

TWENTY-ONE

Cecilia's office. 8:15 a.m. 31ˢᵗ October.

Glyn Davies joined the team meeting the following morning, but indicated that Cecilia was to lead it as usual. After dealing with various routine matters, she turned once more to the 1994 golf club deaths and noted that the DNA testing of current club members had produced no matches for the blood on Farthing's clothes.

"Which," she said, having taken to heart Davies' earlier words to her, "we might have expected. It would be nice if we'd got a match for that blood, but for the moment we're probably going to have to admit that we've learnt what can be learnt from it— which is that someone who wasn't James Farthing was involved in murdering the Kermode boy or at least in moving his corpse, that we'll be able to identify him if we can find him, but that it wasn't any of the present members of the golf club, or any past member that we have access to. So what else do we have? What about those exercise books? Have we found them yet?"

Joseph shook his head. "Verity and I looked carefully. Actually, we scoured the place. There *aren't* any exercise books, or anything like exercise books, in the evidence section for this case. We went through everything. Maybe they got mixed up with something else. I'm going to get the whole area searched later today, as soon as we've got some people free."

Cecilia nodded. "Good. Those books have to be somewhere. We need to see them." She paused. "So what about the officers on the original investigation? Joseph, I'm afraid that's you again! How's it going?"

"I'm chasing up the two constables — Wesson and Smith. They're now both detective chief inspectors with CID in Birmingham. They're out on some exercise at the moment, but we should be able to talk to them later in the week. I'll stay on it."

"Good."

"The bad news is," he said, "I've run into a dead end with Barnwell. Since he retired he's disappeared. But Chief Superintendent Davies has said he'll help with that." He turned to Glyn Davies. "Do you have any word for us there, sir?"

"Nothing conclusive as yet," Davies said. "Timothy Barnwell seems to have been a good officer. He'd had good results. But then for some reason he gave up his career and retired almost immediately after this. In November 1994. After retiring I gather he went abroad. When I know where he went and if he's still alive and whether we can get in touch with him, I'll let you know. Meanwhile, keep on with what you're doing. If you'll allow a suggestion, it might be worthwhile for some of you to take another look at the crime scene. I know you'll be twenty years late, but who knows, you might get lucky! At least it'd give you a feel for the area."

He looked down at the floor for a moment, and sighed. Then he looked back at them.

"So, are we finished here, Detective Superintendent?"

"Yes, sir."

"Then, with your permission, I'd like to take Detective Constable Jarman away for that little project I mentioned."

TWENTY-TWO

The car park at the Alphington Golf and Country Club.
The same day, a little before one in the afternoon.

G lyn Davies had chosen his spot carefully. He was parked where he could see the grand entrance to the club, and he also had a good view of the rest of the car park and the exit.

His mobile phone rang.

"Yes, Jarman. How's it going?"

"In the last hour, while I've nursed half a pint of bitter and a packet of crisps, he's had five large scotches on my certain count. I may actually have missed one, so it could be six. But five for sure! He's getting up now and I think he's getting ready to leave." A pause. "Yes! He is. Shall I follow him?"

"You could leave the bar casually about the same time he does, so as to keep an eye on him. But keep your distance."

"Don't worry sir."

A minute passed. He could hear bar sounds — conversation and the chinking of glasses — over the mobile.

The sounds died away.

Then Jarman's voice again. "He's crossed the hall and he's coming out through the main doors now, sir."

"I see him. Good. Drop back."

Glyn Davies watched as Reeves walked to his car and got into it.

He picked up the other mobile. "Are you there?" he said.

"We're here sir."

"Target vehicle is a black Jaguar XJR. It's moving toward the exit now. You should see it any minute."

Another pause.

The Jaguar was lost to his sight amid trees by the entrance to the car park.

He had a moment of anxiety, but then the voice came over the mobile. "We see it, sir. He's just coming out. We're following."

"Good. Hold back as long as you can. Try to get him on a violation."

There was a brief pause and then a sudden chuckle. "That won't be difficult, sir. He's doing forty-odd already!"

It was technically a built up area, and speed cameras had been installed only weeks previously.

The Chief Superintendent smiled. "Then I trust you will do your duty, Officer," he said.

"Yes, sir!"

He laid aside the mobile, took a deep, pleasurable breath, and sat back.

"Gotcha!" he said softly.

TWENTY-THREE

Heavitree Police Station. 8:30 the following morning.

"But surely, sir—?" Cecilia began when Chief Superintendent Davies gave her the news of Dennis Reeves's arrest—but then she stopped.

"Surely what, Detective Superintendent Cavaliere?"

"Surely we weren't supposed to—I mean, wasn't this because we already knew?"

"As you will notice if you check the Police UK website, Detective Superintendent, speeding has for some time been a priority policing concern in the village of Alphington."

"I see sir," she said doubtfully.

"And so," he continued, "our splendid and ever watchful colleagues in traffic stopped Reeves as a matter of routine. Then when they tested him—as a matter of routine—it turned out that his blood alcohol content was in the stratosphere. So then he was arrested for driving while intoxicated. And that meant—as a matter of routine—that he had to give a DNA sample. And that meant *as a matter of routine* that his DNA went into the national database. And *that* means that those vigilant traffic cops will quite rightly get *all* the credit for catching not just a drunk driver but also a serial rapist. And for better or worse our little operation won't even get a mention. All we get is the satisfaction of knowing that Dennis Reeves won't be raping anyone else. Is that all right by you, Cecilia Cavaliere?"

"Yes, sir. Absolutely, sir."

Chief Superintendent Davies nodded. "Good. I thought it might be." He paused and looked at her. Perhaps she still looked uncomfortable. "You know Cecilia, human justice is seldom perfect. We just have to do the best we can. I'm not suggesting we should ever *break* the law. But just occasionally, when the law seems to leave off at a crucial point, I think we mustn't be too proud or pure to... well... to *improvise* a bit."

TWENTY-FOUR

The President's office in the Alphington Golf and Country Club.
10:15 that morning.

The president's office in the Alphington Golf and Country Club was a splendid room, lofty and spacious, with handsome bookcases and tall windows looking out onto well cared-for lawns and a magnificent group of oak trees that flourished fifty or so meters to the west. The room itself had been the master's study and sanctum in those palmy days when Alphington House was home and seat to the earls of Hatherleigh, vastly wealthy in their time but (being apparently less fecund in bed than at the bank) now extinct. Its furnishing and décor were among only twenty-six commissions known to have been accepted by the great Thomas Chippendale.

But the present occupant was not enjoying it.

John Pinkerton sat sadly in the big chair behind his desk, shaking his head. The news about Dennis Reeves, which Cecilia gathered he'd received earlier that morning, seemed to have affected him deeply.

"I can't believe it," he said. "I mean, I suppose I have to believe it. There's no possibility of a mistake, is there?"

"Not in this case, I don't think so, sir. I understand that when they confronted him he simply admitted it."

"I'd introduced him to my wife, my daughters. We'd *eaten* together. I just don't know what's happening to the world. I just don't understand."

"I'm sorry," Cecilia said. And somewhat to her surprise, she really was.

He looked up at her. "Yes," he said. "I believe you. You're a decent woman. And you're trying to do your job. I see that. I'm afraid I was rude to you the other day. There was no excuse for that. It's just that—no. That doesn't matter. I was rude."

Cecilia gazed at him for a moment.

"Forgive my asking," she said, "but was that by any chance an apology?"

He gave a half smile. "Yes, I think it was. But very awkwardly expressed!"

She nodded. "Then apology accepted," she said gently. After a moment she added, "I don't know if it's any help, but I gather that when they charged Reeves with... with the rapes and so on, he actually seemed quite relieved. Admitted everything straight away. As if he was glad to get it off his chest."

Pinkerton nodded. "Yes, I suppose he might be. If you'd been living a lie all those years, it could be a relief. I can see that." He paused. "And now I understand a team of your lads is going to take another look at the place where all that other stuff happened in '94—near the tenth hole, where they found those poor boys?"

"Yes, sir. I admit, after all this time, the chances of finding anything relevant are minimal. But there's some evidence the original investigation wasn't quite as thorough as it should have been, so we think we ought to give it a try."

"No stone unturned and all that, eh?"

"That's right, sir."

"Good," he said. "That's the ticket. Well, Detective Superintendent, I wish you and your lads luck. I hope the blighter that did it's still around and you can nail him."

"Thank you, sir. We'll do our best!"

She had, it seemed, made a convert.

While she was walking down the steps of the clubhouse, Cecilia had a call on her mobile.

It was Joseph. "About those two officers who worked with Barnwell, Wesson and Smith," he said. "I've been in contact, and we can talk to them together via satellite. They've said they can be available. Shall I set it up? Or do you want to interview them separately?"

Cecilia pursed her lips.

"I think together will be fine," she said finally.

TWENTY-FIVE

"You might get lucky," Glyn Davies had said when he suggested they look again at the crime scenes — and they did.

In fact they had already done so by the time Cecilia arrived. She found her "lads," which was to say, Verity Jones, Headley Jarman, and Tom Wilkins, standing in a small circle in the heavily wooded area — what Headley Jarman referred to as "the jungle" — about thirty meters distant from the notorious "dogleg" on the fairway, and about ten from Abbott's Lane. They were gathered around something that was filthy, rusting, and in a fair way to disintegration but still perfectly recognizable: a boy's bicycle.

"Tom found it under the bushes," Verity said as Cecilia approached. She pointed to where broken branches and disturbed earth marked the spot from which they had extracted it. "It was almost buried and totally overgrown. And cheers for Tom. I'd never have spotted it! I can quite see why they call this part 'the jungle'!"

Headley nodded. "If your ball goes in here you don't bother to look for it, because you'll never get it out even if you find it.

You just settle for the fact you're going to have a bogey, go back to the tee, and reload."

"Uh huh," Verity said, evidently getting the general idea if not quite all the details.

"It's a Raleigh all right," Tom said, crouching and peering at it, "you can still make out the insignia. Look."

Cecilia looked and nodded. Most of the classic Raleigh heron's head badge was visible through the dirt, and beneath it part of the word *Nottingham*.

"I'm pretty sure this bike was black, and it certainly had a Sturmey-Archer three-speed gear," Tom added, pointing to the rusting handlebars. "That all fits the description Kermode's sister gave, doesn't it?"

"It does. Perfectly. It's got to be Frankie's."

He nodded. "It was a good bike. I'd reckon the frame's still salvageable, with some work. And it'd be worth saving. Of course you'd need to replace everything else. But you'd have a great boy's bike at the end of it. A classic."

Cecilia smiled at his enthusiasm. But then—

"If this was here when the boy was murdered," she said, "how on earth did the original investigation manage to overlook it?"

"It's nearly thirty meters from where they found Kermode's body," Tom said, standing up, "and if the boy had decided to take a walk, I dare say he decided to hide his bike anyway. It was highly nickable. And out here it's on the common land between the club's land and the lane. Not technically a part of the golf course at all."

But Cecilia was not in a mood to accept excuses. "That shouldn't have made any difference. And it's no nearer now to where they found Kermode's body than it was twenty years ago. If you could find it after all this time, they should have found it then. And what's that?"

Between the bike and the bushes from which it had come was a metal box.

"Yes, ma'am. I was coming to that," Tom said. "That fell out of what was left of the saddle bag when I dragged the bike out. We haven't touched it. We all thought you'd want to get it back and have the lab open it. Just in case it's important."

Cecilia peered at it. "I'm surprised it isn't rusty. It's dirty, but still looks good under the dirt."

"That's because it's aluminium," Tom said. "That doesn't rust. It's a tight fit—virtually airtight—and it's nice and light for carrying your stuff in."

"Oh," Cecilia said. "Well, I certainly want to know what it's in it. And I'm sure you're right—we'll be smart to contain our impatience and let the lab open it. Let's get it into an evidence bag. Meanwhile this is terrific work. Well done everyone!"

TWENTY-SIX

Heavitree Police Station. That afternoon.

Cecilia had Verity with her downstairs in what Joseph called "the boffins' underground kingdom," as he prepared to bring up Detective Chief Inspectors Wesson and Smith on screen for interview.

"Lo, Detective Chief Inspectors Tweedledum and Tweedledee!" he said.

"What?" Cecilia said.

He grinned. "Just wait and see!"

Given Joseph's introduction, Cecilia and Verity indeed had difficulty keeping straight faces when the two officers appeared on the screen looking plump, cherubic, and cheerful. They managed, however, to contain themselves.

Introductions were made, and the subject of the interview was indicated. Despite their cherubic appearance, the two were good witnesses, and even after twenty years it was evident that they still remembered quite well the case involving Frank Kermode and James Farthing.

"It was our first murder case after we'd both just made it as detective," Wesson said, "so we were pretty keen but also pretty green. And to tell you the truth, we were both really cut up that it was just a kid."

"I hate it when it involves a kid," she'd said soon after she'd become a detective inspector.

"The day you stop hating it, ma'am," Sergeant Wyatt said, "is probably the day to think about retiring."

Dear Sergeant Wyatt! He was retired now. And she missed him.

"Ma'am?"

It was Verity.

"Sorry!" She brought herself abruptly back to the present. "Actually, I'd think less of you if you weren't cut up because it was a kid, and you'd be less good as police officers." She paused. "But granted that awfulness, how else did the inquiry feel? I mean—what was it like, working with Detective Superintendent Barnwell?"

"Tough in a lot of ways," Wesson said. "But that was good for us. Most of the time he was an absolute stickler for detail—had us conducting exhaustive interviews with all the locals, staff at the club, even some of the club members, and was meticulous about recording everything."

"So we've seen," Cecilia said.

"And then—well, you'll have noticed the murder weapon appeared to have been a golf iron."

"We did."

"Well again, Barnwell had us spend hours combing through every single golf club on the premises and in members' homes areas for signs of blood or violence. That was mostly work for us junior detectives and for uniform, though with some of the senior members and their families Barnwell actually went through the stuff himself. He seemed determined to leave nothing to chance. But then—"

He hesitated.

"But then what?"

"Well, to be honest, alongside all that careful work, just once or twice he seemed to us to go to the other extreme and act a bit… well, if I had to put a word on it, I'd say slapdash."

Cecilia raised an eyebrow.

Wesson looked at Smith, who nodded and took up the story.

"That's right. I remember being surprised at how quickly we got through looking at the original crime scene, where Frank Kermode's body was. Admittedly, Barnwell had arrived there before any of us. I suppose he felt he'd seen everything that could be seen. He showed us how it was clear that the body had been dragged from the lane, pointed to the scuff marks on the tops of the boy's shoes, and all that. And of course we respected the fact that he was an experienced officer."

"Even so, you're right," Wesson said. "It *was* surprising how quick he was. I mean, after we'd arrived and he'd filled us in, I did think he'd want us to check around a bit more. But he didn't. Said it was all covered."

"As I think about it now," Smith said, "looking back, I wonder if he was actually starting to burn out a bit—with the job." He looked at Wesson, who nodded. "We do know he retired soon after. And he was getting those nosebleeds."

"He was getting *what*?" Cecilia said.

"Nosebleeds. We put it down to stress."

Wesson nodded. "We did wonder if maybe he was even drinking a bit too much, though neither of us ever smelled alcohol on him during the day."

Cecilia exchanged a glance with Verity.

"Forensics said the spatter pattern on the boy's clothes was a nosebleed," she said. "Didn't that strike you as a bit of a coincidence?"

"I suppose it did. But why on earth would Barnwell have wanted to kill a thirteen-year-old? Anyway, he was a different blood group: A Rhd positive. The blood on the boy's clothes was O Rhd positive."

She nodded. "Right." She paused. "So how did you know Barnwell's blood group?"

"There'd been a blood drive the week before, actually. We all got cards as donors with our blood group on."

"And you saw his card?"

"We did, actually. He'd showed it to us one night in the pub. Very pleased with himself he was! Apparently if he needed blood, ours would do fine for him. But if *we* needed blood, his would kill us!"

She smiled. "I see. Well, that sounds pretty conclusive."

"So then," Verity said, "the day after the body was found, Barnwell pulled in James Farthing as a suspect, didn't he?"

"That's right, he did," Wesson said. "And for a bit that looked promising. The lad had a record, flashing. But then when we interviewed him it seemed to go the other way. We really hadn't any evidence, and personally I liked the boy and began to think he'd had nothing to do with it. But then after we'd let him go without charge he went and committed suicide, which I suppose meant he had a guilty conscience—and showed Barnwell had been right to focus on him, even though he wasn't able to make it stick."

"Tell us about the suicide," Verity said. "You went to that scene, too?"

The two looked at each other.

"Both of us," Smith said. "Barnwell had arrived there right off and sent for us. He seemed to think it was pretty well open and shut."

Wesson nodded. "Quite a little lecture he gave us. 'This is a tragic scene,' he said, 'and there's no point wasting taxpayers' money and indulging our own curiosities when it's perfectly obvious what has happened. For decency's sake, and out of consideration for the poor boy's parents, let's get the body taken down and back to the morgue as soon as possible.'"

"So you two didn't look closely at the body in situ? Before it was taken down?"

"No, not at all," Smith said. "Barnwell had covered that. Do you remember he even got mad at the photographer?"

"Oh, yes," Wesson said, "the photographer! He arrived and started photographing the lad hanging there—not touching anything, mind, keeping his distance, all quite correct—while Barnwell was dealing with something else—I can't remember what, maybe a reporter. Anyway, when Barnwell realized he was clicking away he got really mad at him. Practically accused him of being a weirdo, getting a kick out of photographing corpses, that sort of thing."

"Which did seem hard," Smith said. "So far as we could see, the poor bloke was just trying to do his job."

Wesson nodded. "But then," he added, "to be fair to Barnwell, he *had* arrived on the scene before anyone else and I suppose he thought he'd seen all there was to see and didn't want to make things worse for the poor lad's parents. God knows things were bad enough! His dad worked as groundskeeper at the golf club, you know."

Cecilia nodded. "You don't happen to know who the photographer was, do you?"

They looked at each other.

"It was old Jimmy Ringrose, wasn't it?" Wesson said.

"That's right. He retired the next year, and that was when Keith Berryman came on."

Good Lord, had Keith Berryman been here that long? Apparently he had, though he still looked to Cecilia as if he could scarcely be out of school.

"You won't be able to interview him though—Jimmy Ringrose, I mean," Wesson added, anticipating her next question. "He died a couple of years back. But his photos should still be in the file."

Cecilia exchanged a look with Verity and sighed. "So

Detective Superintendent Barnwell was at both scenes before anyone else, was he?" she said. "The body in the ditch *and* the suicide? That was very efficient of him."

"Ah, well, he played there more or less every day."

"He did? Really?"

"Yes. He wasn't a member, but they'd given him member's privileges, or something like that."

"I see."

Cecilia and Verity looked at each other again, and Cecilia raised an eyebrow. That Barnwell himself actually had a rather close relationship with the Alphington club was not, apparently, something he'd thought worth mentioning in his reports.

"So," Wesson continued, "if word came to the clubhouse of an accident or an incident, if Detective Superintendent Barnwell was there, naturally he'd be the first to hear about it and get to the scene. And that's what had happened when they found Farthing's body — the suicide. He was up at the clubhouse so he went down to investigate."

Cecilia nodded. "Yes, I see that. Naturally that's what would happen.... By the way, you said that when you were checking golf clubs, Barnwell checked through some of the sets himself. Do you remember whose, in particular?"

They looked at each other.

"We certainly did most of them," Wesson said. "Let's see, I think he did young Farthing's set — which wasn't his, actually, but lent him by the club."

"And he did the other lad's. The captain's son — what was his name?"

"Caitlyn — no, Catesby, that was it. He did the two youngsters. And we did all the others."

"And both of their sets were all present and correct?"

"So we understood."

"Thank you."

"You thought for a minute there that Barnwell himself might be in the frame," Verity said when the interview was over.

Cecilia shrugged. "It crossed my mind. But if his blood group was different from that on the boy, then the nosebleed thing *must* have been just a coincidence. And I dare say Wesson had a point: why on earth would Barnwell have *wanted* to kill a thirteen-year-old?" She considered, then said, "But what is getting clearer and clearer to me is that Barnwell's investigation was a mess. I think DCI Smith is right—Barnwell was burning out. And Jenny Farthing is certainly right: her son didn't get justice."

TWENTY-SEVEN

The team was already gathered in Cecilia's office.

"I don't know," Cecilia said, "what kind of records the Alphington golf club keeps of which people play on the course and when, or how long they keep them, but I'd like us to look into it. Do they have to book? Presumably they can't all play at once! How does it work? Verity, could you look into that—and Headley, maybe you could help her with golf-speak, if that's a problem. The point is, if it's possible to find out, I'd like to know if who was booked to play on the days when they found the bodies, and who they were playing with, and anything else you can find about who was there and when. I'd like to see how far any club records square with the statements they all made."

Verity and Headley looked at each other and nodded.

"We're onto it," Verity said.

Cecilia's phone rang.

"Good morning." It was Tom Foss, from the laboratory.

"Hang on." She put the call on speaker. "So what have we got? Anything we can use?"

"Well, more than you'd think. Actually, if you insist on leaving your stuff out in the woods for twenty years and want it to be in reasonable nick at the end of it, then an aluminium box isn't at all a bad choice to put it in."

"All right. So what's in it?"

"Mostly pens and pencils. A Casio electronic calculator, state of the art for 1994, and a school exercise book. And it's got a name on the cover. Frank Kermode."

"Can we read it?"

"You soon will be able to. There's no great problem really. It was dry and brittle, and of course it had been folded for twenty years! So I'm humidifying it. I'd like to give it a three or four more hours. Then I dare say we can open it without any problems."

"Okay."

"And *then* what I suggest is, instead of all you heavy-fingered plods thumbing it through and it falling to pieces under the assault, you let us scientific types with our delicate and sensitive touch scan the pages for you and upload the scans to your computers. We can do that for you by tomorrow morning. That way you'll be able to read it just as well as you could the original—maybe more easily. And you can all read it at once at your very own desks on your very own laptops! *And* you'll still have the original if you want to check anything."

"Thanks Tom! We owe you."

"Your profound gratitude and everlasting indebtedness are assumed."

"Yes, well don't push it."

When he had rung off she looked at the others. "So maybe we finally have hold of one of those elusive exercise books that Joan Kermode was talking about." She paused, speculatively. "I'd still like to know where the rest of them are, though."

"One's better than none," Verity said, cheerfully stating the obvious.

"So are we finished for the moment?" Cecilia said. "Is there anything else?"

Verity and Joseph looked at each other.

"Actually," Joseph said, "we think there might be."

"Go on."

"It's about James Farthing's suicide. It started with something Verity noticed." He looked at her.

"When I read the forensic reports," she said, "it seemed to me that there was an anomaly about James Farthing's suicide. The report suggested that at some time before his death he'd had a bang on the head. Not enough to kill him, but probably enough to stun him. Of course the report didn't know just how *long* before, so it *could* have been nothing to do with his death—which is presumably why the investigation didn't make anything of it. But then when I considered that the other boy's death *also* began with his being stunned, it set me to wondering. And when I told Joseph of my wondering, he started to wonder too. And now it's your turn," she said, turning to her husband. "Tell them the fruits of your wondering!"

"Right!" Joseph indicated the photographs of the suicide on the second white board. "Let's start by looking again at these. They were shot on medium speed 35mm film with a 50mm lens, and they're good—lots of detail. And now please look at this."

He produced an enlarged section of one of the pictures already on the whiteboard and attached it.

"From the photo of the lad hanging," he said, "I'm giving you here a blowup of the rope over the branch. What do you see?"

They peered.

"A deep groove in the bark," Headley said after a moment. "Deeper than I'd have expected."

The others nodded.

"And the rope hanging down beyond the branch, on the other side?" Joseph said, "Away from the body? What about that?"

"It's stained," Tom said. "From the tree? The bark? As it was dragged over?"

"Presumably," Headley said. "It looks woody and mossy."

But then—

"Oh!" Cecilia said suddenly.

The others looked at her.

"It's going the wrong way," she said. "That's your point, isn't it?"

Joseph nodded. "Yes. When Farthing killed himself, he'd surely have had to climb up somehow, throw the rope over the branch and fasten it, and *then* let himself fall. If the rope had been dragged over the branch at all, it would have dragged *towards* him, on his side. But that rope was dragged over the branch *away* from him, with a heavy weight on it. In which case?"

"*He* was the weight," Cecilia said, "and someone *else* was doing the dragging. Which means he didn't commit suicide at all. He was murdered."

Silence.

"And here," Joseph continued, producing a large plastic evidence bag, "is the rope. This *was* still in evidence. I collected it after we'd finished looking for the exercise books. It seems to me to confirm everything the photograph indicates. See those stains—from the bark. Look at the way the rope's fiber's been pressed—*toward* the noose, still evident even after twenty years. It was dragged over the branch, with the weight on the noose, as you said. But look for yourselves."

They peered at it in the plastic evidence bag.

There was another moment of silence.

"Which now," Verity said, "gives us quite a different scenario from the one we've been thinking about. James Farthing was first stunned, and then someone hanged him while he was unconscious."

"So," Cecilia said, "what Barnwell was actually dealing

with wasn't a murder and a suicide but two murders, surely connected to each other: in fact surely committed by the same person."

The others nodded.

"We even have something of an MO," Headley said. "The murderer stuns his victims from behind, then kills them while they're unconscious."

"Right," Cecilia said. She turned back to Joseph and Verity. "This is terrific work. Thanks to you two, I think we've just taken a quantum leap." She paused. "Now, I'm wondering about a step even further. Would I be right in thinking that if anyone actually pulled on this rope, *gripped* it so as to be able to pull hard, hard enough to lift a body, there might be some trace of their DNA left on it, even after twenty years?"

"There *might* be something," Joseph said, "provided they didn't wear gloves—but please put a big emphasis on *might*! The problem is, God knows how the thing's been handled in those twenty years since, or who handled it. It's a long shot."

"Even so, I'd like you to tell the lab to take that shot. I know you can't promise anything, but I want to know if there is still *any* evidence on that rope as to who may have pulled it, or who may have handled it, twenty years ago."

"I'll get them on to it."

"What I don't understand," Tom said, looking again at the photographs, "is why Barnwell didn't notice any of this to start with. I mean—he was looking at the original scene, and it ought surely to have been pretty obvious to an experienced police officer."

"According to DCIs Wesson and Smith," Verity said, "he hardly bothered to look at it at all, and discouraged anyone else. Even they called it slapdash."

Cecilia nodded. "I'm afraid it fits the pattern we're seeing more and more. It's fair enough that in 1994 Barnwell didn't do what we now routinely do with bloodstains. I'm even willing to concede that deciding Frank Kermode's 'detecting' was unimportant or that there was no point in searching further afield for clues at the original murder site were judgment calls—though I think bad ones. But this is different. I agree with you, Tom. This didn't need twenty-first century technology or even insightful judgment. All it needed was good old-fashioned observation. This was sheer incompetence."

TWENTY-EIGHT

Cecilia's office at Heavitree Police Station. The following morning.

"So what we now want to know," Cecilia said to the team gathered in her office, "is who are Mrs. F and Major C?"

"Or were," Verity said. "They might be dead."

"Right. Or were."

Tom Foss had been as good as his word, and the contents of Frank Kermode's exercise book had duly arrived that morning ready to be viewed on their computer screens: schoolboy writing, but clear enough even after twenty years. And Foss was surely right: it had to be easier to read than the original, if only because one could increase the size and improve the contrast.

Even so, it hardly made for riveting reading.

The boy had had, indeed, a fascination with writing down where he saw people and when he saw them and what he saw them doing that amounted to a fixation. And most of what he had seen and recorded those twenty years ago was, so far as they could see, of no interest whatever:

Tuesday 10.27 a.m. Mrs. T at the post office. 11 mins. Bought stamps.

10.44. Mrs T at the butchers. Bought 2 lamb chops

And so on.

And on.

Page after page detailing ten days of comings and goings in the life of an English village from the twenty-third of June to the second of July in 1994 — a mine of what was, from their point of view, utterly useless information. Save perhaps for one group of references. Somebody called *"Major C"* had paid repeated visits over those ten days to a *"Mrs. F,"* and this had obviously been a matter of peculiar fascination to the would-be detective, who had marked his observations in this connection with stars, asterisks, and exclamation marks.

"It sounds to me," Headley said, "as if another trip around the older folk in the village might be useful. If this Major C and Mrs. F were having a hot and heavy fling, surely someone else besides young Frank noticed and might remember?"

Cecilia nodded. "Right. Can you and Tom get onto that this afternoon?"

The two young officers looked at each other and grinned.

"There's the Lamb and Flag," Tom said. "We could start there. I'm told they do an excellent steak and kidney pie. And at lunchtime lots of old boys from the Royal British Legion go round there, which should help."

Cecilia stared at him. "Why?"

"British Legion," he said. *"Ex-forces!* Major C sounds to me as if he was army."

Cecilia nodded. "I get it."

Tom looked at his watch. "We can just be there in nice time if we leave now."

"And over a pint," Headley said, "who knows what dark and sexy secrets those hoary bosoms may reveal?"

TWENTY-NINE

The Lamb and Flag public house, Alphington.
12:15 p.m. the same day.

The landlord checked the glass before filling it, and chuckled. "Oh, yes," he said, proceeding to pull a half pint. "I think I can tell you who *Mrs. F* and *Major C* were all right. That would be Mrs. Fletcher and Major Catesby. They were at it for years. Everyone knew. Well, everyone but poor Mrs. Catesby."

"Catesby?" Headley said, "Was he related to the Catesby who's at the golf club now—Greg Catesby, the membership secretary and treasurer?"

"Yes, of course he was. That's his son."

The landlord handed them their half pints of Badger Best, and they paid.

There was a moment of silence and proper respect while they sampled and expressed satisfaction.

"So," Tom said, "the present membership secretary and treasurer's dad was knocking off this Mrs. Fletcher bird?"

"That's right. He—that's Major Catesby, the dad—was club captain, back then. Terribly upper class! And awfully army, don't you know! Always insisted on being called 'Major,' even when he'd retired. Pompous prat!"

"So Catesby senior was a soldier?"

"He *had* been a soldier — of sorts. Actually, there was a bit of a thing about that, too."

"A thing?"

"Well, the Major was military all right. And the story was, he'd been due to ship out to the Falklands in '82. Third Commando Brigade it would have been. But then guess what! He suddenly has a very convenient knee injury. Can't go! There were some raised eyebrows about that, I can tell you. So the upshot of it was that while the rest of the lads were out there in the middle of a south Atlantic winter thousands of miles from home, pulling off a miracle with lousy equipment and poor rations against a numerically superior enemy who was dug in before they even got there, our gallant Major Catesby was boldly flying a mahogany bomber in Whitehall. Nice work if you can get it! You talk to some of the lads." He nodded towards a group of elderly men gathered round a table at far the end of the bar, waiting for their helpings of steak and kidney pudding. "Quite a few of them were in the Falklands. And they've not got a lot to say that's good about our Major Catesby."

"So what happened to him then?"

"Catesby? He retired from the army soon after the Falklands. Well, did he jump or was he pushed? Anyway, he wasn't in the army any more. Of course, the family is richer than God, so he never *needed* to do anything. And he became club captain at the Golf Club, like I said. Bossed everyone around there. Until the accident."

"The accident?"

"He and his missus got killed in a car crash — 1995, if I remember rightly. Nasty smash. Went off the road into a tree. Doing eighty or so and they were almost out of petrol, so the tank was full of fumes. The thing blew up. She was driving. Killed them both. But don't get me wrong. She was a nice lady. Everyone liked her. Her only mistake — apart from driving into a tree at eighty miles an hour of course — was marrying him. Fortunately for the rest of us the son — Greg Catesby — takes after her rather than him. No side at all. Quite often comes in for a pint."

"So he's all right, is he?"

"Oh, yes, always has a good word for everybody. You couldn't find a nicer bloke. And of course he does a lot of good." He indicated a "Save the Children" box on the counter by the beer handles. "That's his lot. Spends hours a week working for them, he does — serves in the shop on Paris Street. You can always find him there on Fridays."

"So who was this Mrs. Fletcher the major was having it off with then?"

"Wife of the bank manager. Hot stuff she was, if you like that sort of thing. Major Catesby was all over her. As I say, everyone knew about it. Everyone except Mrs. Catesby."

"And is Mrs. Fletcher still around?"

"Oh yes, very much so. It's the big house on Carlton Crescent. The Gables. I think it's number eight. Set back from the road, with white pillars. You can't miss it. She's still there. She's a widow now."

Presumably a merry widow, Headley thought.

"I think," he said when they were outside in the car park about half an hour later, having eaten their steak and kidney pie and chatted up some of the local veterans, who all told much the same story as the landlord, "that we might continue our afternoon's work with a visit to Carlton Crescent."

"I think I agree with you," Tom said.

THIRTY

"We looked into those who played on the Alphington course on the days you asked about," Verity said as she and Cecilia walked out to lunch. "To book a round on the course, they just write their names in a time slot in a big diary — first come, first served. It's a simple system, but seems to work well enough. Which is no doubt why they've been doing it for years. The problem from our point of view is that they chuck the old books away once the year is passed, so there's no way of checking on detail for 1994. That's the bad news."

"Which sounds as if there might be some good news?" Cecilia said.

"The good news is, we chatted to Glossop, an aged retainer who has been serving the club forever, has eyes in his head, and clearly uses them. His recollection, and I incline to trust it, is that on the day before they discovered Frank Kermode's body — in other words, on the day when the boy was actually killed — there was hardly anyone out on the course at all. The place was pretty well empty: club house, everything. Apparently there was some kind of local jamboree for golfers at the Exeter club, and a lot of them were at that. And Major Catesby the club captain was at some big golf-meeting thing in Scotland. Anyway, as he recalls, young Gregory Catesby did play a solitary round just for practice, and he went out at about eleven. And then Detective Superintendent Barnwell turned up to play a solitary round a bit later, and he went out at about twelve. Barnwell must have caught Catesby up, though, because Glossop noticed that they came back together."

Cecilia nodded thoughtfully. "He remembers a lot, for such a long time ago."

"Yes, he does, and of course he may be misremembering, or remembering things he doesn't really remember so as to please me! But it was obviously a time that stuck in his memory because of all that happened afterwards, and I have to say he's an impressive old man in a quiet way. So despite the maybes, I think it's also possible his recollection might be more or less right."

"What about the day when James Farthing's body was found?"

"As it happened Glossop wasn't there that day, so he can't help with that, and so far we can't find anyone else who remembers anything about it beyond what we already know. There were a couple of other club servants about—but they were older men, and they've both gone to their rewards. So no joy for us there. I did get chatting to Greg Catesby though, and he did his best to be helpful."

"Yes?"

"He took me into his office and helped me go through their old member records on his computer. He's turned up a couple more people who were members in 1994 and moved away since. I've got their details, so I'll try to contact them over the next few days and see if they can add anything."

Cecilia nodded.

"All right. Well, do what you can. Every little helps."

THIRTY-ONE

The Gables, Carlton Crescent. About 2:00 p.m. the same day.

"You boys are sure you won't have a drink?"

"No, thank you, Mrs. Fletcher," Tom said.

"You're very kind, ma'am, but it's considered bad form on duty," Headley added.

Mrs. Fletcher smiled and shook her head. "God, you're all so *virtuous* these days!"

Or perhaps, Tom thought, it's just that we're even more intimidated by DSI Cavaliere than we are by you.

"Well you'll have to forgive me if I have one," Mrs. Fletcher said, and topped her glass up generously from a crystal decanter. "I did give up booze once. That was some years ago." She chuckled. "I think it was the worst day of my life!"

She sat down with her drink on the sofa opposite them, crossed her legs—which, Tom had to admit, were pretty good, considering she had to be in her fifties—and arranged her green and gold skirt.

"You have to understand, booze is my only vice," she said. "Well, unless you count smoking and sex. I suppose,"—she reached for a gold case on the table beside her—"you're the same about cigarettes?"

They both smiled and shook their heads.

"I was afraid you might be."

She lit a cigarette, drew on it deeply, and exhaled.

"That's better," she said. "Now, in answer to your question: as an all round human being, Henry Catesby was a bit of a wanker. But he was pretty good in bed. Not as good as he thought he was, of course — few men are — but pretty good. And he was certainly an improvement on my husband, though I admit that's not saying much. The only thing that ever got Samuel Fletcher up at night was his bladder!"

"So your husband — Mr. Fletcher — was still alive at the time?"

"That's right. He didn't die until 1998. July, if I remember rightly. Mind you, it took several days before most people noticed. He was that kind of man. Some of us thought he'd been dead for years."

"So you and Major Catesby were in a relationship in 1994?" Headley said.

She laughed. "'In a relationship'! God, sweetie, you sound like a Victorian novel! Yes, I suppose we were. Which in plain English meant, *he* regularly needed a good screw to make up for his prissy wife — who was Catholic and I think talked about sex as 'rendering him his debt' or some such crap — and *I* was happy to be it — the good screw, I mean."

"So," — Headley referred to his notes, wherein he'd written the dates that had been specified for Major C and Mrs. F's assignations in Frank Kermode's exercise book — "it's quite likely you and Major Catesby would have been together on the afternoons of 23rd June to 2nd July 1994?"

Again she laughed. "I should think it's highly likely, though we weren't exactly keeping records, you know. I'd just call him on his mobile at that golf club of his and say, 'The bore's at the bank, so you can come round,' or something like that, and round he'd come. But that was most afternoons, I can tell you."

"Yet you called the major a bit of wanker, Mrs. Fletcher,"

Tom said. "That's not a very flattering way to talk about your lover. Why was he a bit of a wanker?"

"My *lover*? I don't think that's the word I'd use. Henry was good enough in bed, as I said, but I wouldn't have trusted him any other way, not further than I could throw him."

"Was there any particular way that he let you down personally?" Headley asked.

"Not me! I was too smart to give him the chance. But you could take it as given he'd always do whatever suited him best. He was cheating on his wife, after all."

"You were cheating on your husband, weren't you?"

She gave a half smile. "I never said I was an angel, sweetie. You asked about Major Catesby. Henry Catesby and I had an arrangement that suited us both. I suppose we trusted each other that far. But if ever it hadn't suited either of us that would have been the end of it. Simple as that."

There was a pause.

"Did you ever sense that Major Catesby might be violent, Mrs. Fletcher?"

She drew on her cigarette, considering. "Well yes, maybe there was a streak of that in him. I dare say he could be a bit of a bully. He never tried it on with me, though."

"If you sensed that, didn't it scare you at all?"

She smiled and shook her head. "You know, sweetie, I didn't grow up with all this," —she waved a bejeweled hand at the well appointed living room — "I married Samuel Fletcher for his money, and as my side of the deal I gave him what he wanted, which was a very decorative ornament to show off at dinners with his banking pals. But aside from all that, I suppose I was what you might call a tough little whore. Which means, I knew how to look after myself if I had to. I still do."

Tom exchanged a glance with Headley, who nodded. Evidently they had the same thought.

"Mrs. Fletcher," Headley asked, taking the bull by the horns, "do you have any idea as to Major Catesby's whereabouts in the early afternoon of the first of September, 1994?"

She laughed. "Come on now!" she said. "If you want an intelligent answer you're going to have to do better than that. Quite probably he was in bed with me! Just like all the other dates you asked about. But it was twenty-odd years ago, for God's sake! I told you—I don't keep records! So the absolute truth is, I don't know. What was so special about the first of September?"

"It was the day a boy from the village was murdered," Tom said.

"Oh." She frowned, and placed her glass on the table beside her. "You mean the kid they found by the golf course? In a ditch? Beaten to death?"

"That's right. They found his body on the second of September. But forensics established that he'd been killed twenty-four hours earlier, in the early afternoon of the first."

"And you think Henry did it?"

"If he was with you he couldn't have, could he?" Headley said. "We're just asking questions, Mrs. Fletcher."

She stared at them. "Well," she said slowly, "I *do* remember about that kid being murdered. How could I forget? Poor little bugger!" She drew on her cigarette. "And no," she said finally, "as it happens Henry wasn't with me that day, the day before they found the body. He'd been up in Scotland for virtually the whole of the previous week at the Royal and Ancient. There was some kind of conference. They'd invited golf club captains from all over the country. And on that day he was travelling back on the train. I don't think he got back to Alphington until midafternoon. Anyway, I never saw him that day at all."

She paused, thoughtfully.

"But what about the other boy—the seventeen-year-old—who committed suicide afterwards?" she said. "Wasn't that virtually a confession? Why are you still interested in all this?"

"We have new evidence, Mrs. Fletcher. The other boy didn't commit suicide. He was murdered too, just like the first one."

"Jesus Christ! That's terrible." She paused and drew on her cigarette again. "And you mean to say the police have only just caught on to this—after twenty-odd years—that you had two murders on your hands instead of a murder and a suicide? That doesn't say much for your original investigation, does it?"

"No, Mrs. Fletcher, it doesn't," Tom said.

She shook her head. "Well anyway, Henry was on the train on his way back from Scotland on the day when the first boy was killed." She drew on her cigarette again and stared past them, seeming to consider. Then she looked back at them. "At least, that's what he told *me* he was doing. I mean, I didn't exactly bother to check up on him, did I?"

THIRTY-TWO

So was it possible that Major Henry Catesby was the killer they were looking for?

"If he'd found out about Frank Kermode's 'detecting' his affair with Mrs. Fletcher, he'd have had a motive," Joseph said.

"A pretty feeble motive," Verity said. "It was 1994, not 1894! And anyway, half the village seems to have known. He must have realized it wasn't a secret. So was he planning to kill them all?"

"I thought we'd decided that this killing was frenzied and irrational," Joseph said. "So we're looking for a motive or provocation that might seem trivial or irrational to most people? Isn't that what we're doing?"

"All right, maybe we are," Verity said. "But it still can't have been Major Catesby. The DNA on the boy's clothes isn't his."

"How do we know that?" Joseph said. "We don't have the major's DNA."

"We've got his son's," she said. "If it was his father's blood on the boy's clothes, the DNA pattern would be 50 per cent the same."

"What if the major *wasn't* Greg's father?" Joseph said. "He obviously liked to cheat, so maybe Mrs. Catesby did too?"

"That doesn't sound like anything we've heard so far about the woman," Cecilia said, having listened to the discussion up to this point in silence. "But then," —she hesitated—"stranger things have happened. I suppose it's possible."

"Well, all right," Verity said. "For the sake of your hypothesis let us grant *both* these unlikely proposals. Just *possibly* this somewhat feeble motive made Major Catesby go barmy and become a killer. And just *possibly* the DNA on the boy's clothes being all wrong doesn't prove the major didn't move the body because just *conceivably* (clever play on words, of course, intended) seventeen years earlier Mrs. Catesby had it off with a mystery lover. *Even so*, the major *still* can't have murdered Frank Kermode. He had an alibi."

And indeed he had. Mrs. Fletcher may not have checked on Major Catesby's whereabouts, but Cecilia's team had. The Royal and Ancient had records of a weeklong conference that he had indeed attended in 1994, from Thursday the twenty-sixth of August until the following Wednesday evening. His signature appeared on the record of every one of its meetings, every day. The St. Andrews police were very co-operative, not only checking the Royal and Ancient's records but also arranging a satellite interview for Cecilia and her team with an older member of a Scottish club, who had attended that same conference and remembered Major Catesby quite well: "a pleasant enough Englishman, though somewhat opinionated."

St. Andrews police also checked at the prestigious hotel in Old Station Road where Henry Catesby had stayed, and fixed up for Cecilia and her colleagues a second satellite interview, this time with a now senior member of the hotel staff, a still handsome woman in her forties who had been a maid at the hotel in 1994 and remembered Major Catesby well—indeed, as they gathered in the course of their conversation with her, perhaps rather better than well.

"He was more than a wee bit full of himself but quite generous," she said. "I certainly had nothing to complain about and I *know for a fact* he stayed here all night and every night during the week he was in St. Andrews."

Even viewed over the satellite screen, there was surely a reminiscent twinkle in her eye as she said this, and Cecilia for one felt no need to press her on the subject. As Headley put it after the conversation was over, "We already knew Henry Catesby liked to play away from home. It looks like he was also up for the occasional international!"

So it was established beyond reasonable doubt that throughout the week of the conference, Major Catesby had indeed been where he was supposed to be — more or less.

But the crucial day was, of course, the first of September, the day of the murder, the day when he returned home to Exeter. Could he have been back in time to do it?

The elderly Scottish club member remembered at least the start of Major Catesby's day. After an early breakfast, he told them, he drove the major from St. Andrews to Edinburgh Waverley Station, in good time for him to catch the 7:07 a.m. train to Exeter. He reckoned he had deposited Catesby at the station at about ten to seven. Joseph nodded, and checked the timetable. Assuming Catesby took the 7:07, he would not have reached Exeter St. David's until 2:40 p.m., and even then he could hardly have been in Alphington at the golf club before 3:00 p.m., which was no good. If forensics were even approximately right as to the time of death, it was too late for him to have committed the murder.

But Joseph did not sometimes refer to himself as "obsessive compulsive" for nothing. Suppose, he suggested, Major Catesby had cheated? Suppose he only pretended to take the train to Exeter, and then flew back instead?

"So," Verity said, "we are now suggesting that this frenzied attack for which there was little or no rational motive may also have been carefully planned so that the perpetrator had an alibi?"

"You said yourself we should concentrate for the moment on means and opportunity and only afterwards ask about motive."

Verity blew out her cheeks and shook her head.

So *could* the major have been back in time to do it? Was it actually physically possible? There'd been two scheduled flights that morning between Edinburgh Airport and Exeter Airport. Given the witness placed him at Waverley Station shortly before seven, he had already missed the earlier flight, Flybe Flight 290, which was at 6:50 a.m. But he could still have caught the second, Flybe Flight 210 at 10:10 a.m., and that would have had him back in Exeter at 11:45 a.m. — in excellent time to commit the murder! Hot on the trail, Joseph checked with the airline. The Flybe representative was helpful. It was a long time ago but yes, they still had the manifests; they kept these things indefinitely these days.

Joseph waited hopefully while she checked on the computer.

But no one of Major Catesby's name had been on that flight.

Could he have travelled under an assumed name?

Perhaps he could have done that — but wait a minute! The representative didn't know if it mattered, but she noticed that Flybe 210 had been affected by technical problems on that day. There had been an instrument failure. As a result the flight had departed three hours late, and landed at Exeter Airport at 2:45 p.m. Did that make any difference to anything?

Of course it did! It ruined his whole theory. If Major Catesby had been on Flybe 210 that day, he would have arrived in Exeter five minutes later than if he had gone by train! Damn!

Naturally, Joseph (whose manners were impeccable) did not say, "Damn!" to the Flybe representative. He thanked her for her help, replaced the phone, and said it to himself.

Verity drank some tea from her big blue and white striped mug and said nothing.

But wait! Could the wretched man have *chartered* a flight? Now clutching at straws, Joseph checked with the airport, half-knowing the answer before he even heard it. There had been no charters of any kind on the morning of the first of September 1994.

Thank you, you've been very helpful.

He sat back in his chair and closed his eyes. He had to admit it. Unless the St. Andrews police and all their witnesses and all the people he'd just checked with were either suffering from selective amnesia or else lying through their teeth — neither of which seemed likely, however much it might suit him — then even he really could not see any way that Major Catesby could have been back in Exeter in time to kill the boy.

"All right," he said after a minute. "I'm done. I've given it my best shot. Sorry. Major Catesby can't have done it."

Verity had by now perched herself on the desk beside his computer. She gazed down at him fondly.

"That's what I told you to start with," she said.

THIRTY-THREE

St. Mary's Rectory. Late that evening.

It was a time of day that Michael always enjoyed.

Being the fifth of November, traditionally "Guy Fawkes' night," there had been a few fireworks in honour of (or contempt for, depending on your point of view) the gunpowder-plotting recusant of 1605, but they'd been some distance away and they'd stopped now. Figaro hadn't seemed even to notice. People seemed these days to be making more of Halloween a few days earlier. Personally, Michael wasn't crazy about either celebration, though he could quite see why the police and the emergency services would rather have people prancing about in weird costumes pretending to be vampires and witches than letting off fireworks and lighting bonfires.

The night was cold and wet (which was no doubt also part of the reason why there'd been so few fireworks) but inside the rectory was warm and welcoming. Rachel and Rosina had been fed and bathed and were now safely asleep, and Figaro had been taken for his last walk of the day and then retired to continue his watch over them.

So now Michael and Cecilia were alone, wrapped up together in a pleasant bundle on the sofa.

"So what have you been up to?" she said, and he told her — at least, the less totally boring bits, if not necessarily the least ridiculous.

The cheese-ball saga (embarrassing though it was to admit it) had been worrying him for several days. What if he had made the wrong choice and they didn't sell this year? What if the mission committee were left with hundreds of the things? It was as well, he reflected, that he had not gone into politics and had to decide something important — whether or not to involve the country in a war. If cheese-balls so preoccupied him, what on earth would he have done if he'd ever had to make a *real* decision?

In the event, however, it turned out that his anxieties had been unnecessary.

The rector's cheese balls (whether because he had truly made a good choice or merely because people were being nice to him) were selling well, and seemed likely to break last year's record. Even Mrs. Frobisher, widow of Her Britannic Majesty's some-time ambassador to Bolivia, a woman of whose disapproval Michael was always vaguely conscious (he had the impression she regarded him as rather risqué, possibly because he was too high church, or perhaps because he was married to an Italian police officer who was not always in church on Sunday) — even the mighty Mrs. Frobisher had seemed on this occasion to approve, and after the committee meeting had smiled upon him from beneath an enormous hat.

All this Cecilia listened to gravely.

"And what about you?" he said when he had finished.

So she told him the story of the day's investigations — in particular of the amorous Major Catesby and his escapades, and how Joseph had had him in his sights and how it had all come to nothing.

"Poor Joseph," she said. "He really tried to make it work. But it wouldn't." She paused. "And of course, if he *had* somehow managed to pull it off and show a possible link—"

"As he often does," Michael observed. "Think how he and Verity spotted that James Farthing's death wasn't suicide!"

"Exactly! Well, then we'd all have been cheering."

"All the same, what an odd tawdry chap that Major Catesby fellow was, even if he wasn't a murderer!" Michael said. "And if you don't mind me saying so, your fellow Barnwell seems to have been about as much use in his investigating as a hole in the head!"

"We'd noticed that! The whole thing was really incompetent."

"Are you sure it was just incompetence? How many other cases do you know of where the criminal and the police officer investigating it both suffer from nosebleeds?"

"None, actually! But it can't have been Barnwell who bled over the boy. He wasn't the same blood group."

"How do you know that?"

"Smith and Wesson told us."

"And how do *they* know it?"

"He told them."

"*He* told them?"

"He showed them his blood donor card, too. In the pub."

"Did he? That sounds as if he wanted to be awfully sure they got the message."

She pursed her lips and hesitated. "I suppose it does."

"I wonder *why* he'd want be sure of that?"

She said nothing.

"There in the pub," he said, "all supping their pints of beer and being jolly together, are you sure that those two young, inexperienced junior constables actually *examined* the card their senior officer was showing them? Are you certain they couldn't have been deceived in some way?"

Cecilia sat up and stared at him. "Actually, I'm not."

He nodded. "Oh. Well, I just wondered."

THIRTY-FOUR

St. Mary's Rectory. The following morning, 5:15 a.m.

As was her habit when something was bothering her, Cecilia got up early the next morning, made herself coffee — a long dark *Americano* — and then sat with it in an armchair in front of the French windows in the living room, drinking and thinking while the sun rose.

"It sounds as if he wanted to be awfully sure they got they got the message. I wonder why? Are you certain they couldn't have been deceived in some way?"

There'd been a time when was she was fifteen or sixteen, and she and Papa were reading *Othello* together. Suddenly she could take no more. She stopped in the middle of a scene. "This is terrible!" she said, scarcely able to speak, she was so angry. "Othello is supposed to be an intelligent man. What's the matter with him? He says he loves Desdemona. But he believes Iago's lies when Iago hasn't proved anything at all! That's just stupid. She deserves better than that!"

"You're right," Papa said gently. "But I think we have to understand that Othello and Iago are soldiers. They've been in action together. They've stood side by side under fire. That means there's a tremendous bond between them. And that's why Othello is so easily fooled. It simply never occurs to him that his comrade in arms could betray him. He never even considers it. Of course that doesn't make what he does right. He commits a terrible wrong, unspeakable, and in the end he knows it. But it does make him understandable, and perhaps forgivable."

The truth was, of course she'd noticed the nosebleed coincidence from the moment Wesson and Smith mentioned it. "It crossed your mind Barnwell might be in the frame," Verity had said to her straight after the interview, and Verity had been right.

Yet she'd dismissed it. Or rather, she'd simply assumed they *knew* Barnwell's blood group was different from that of the probable killer. But as Michael pointed out, they didn't *know* anything of the kind.

And if any one else involved in the affair had been reported to her as suffering from nosebleeds, she'd surely have pressed much harder? What was she always saying was the first rule of detection? "What we can't show we don't know!" She'd have wanted to check whether Wesson and Smith could have been wrong or deceived. So why hadn't she done that in this case? There were, after all, so *many* elements in Barnwell's handling of the case that were unsatisfactory, and she'd been content to put them all down to incompetence: incompetence in an officer not previously known as incompetent. Why hadn't she looked at once for some more sinister motive?

It wasn't, of course, that she didn't think police officers could be crooked. She was hardly so naïve as that! She'd not forgotten DI Tern or former Chief Superintendent Hanlon. Yet the truth was, she'd disliked and suspected both those men even before she knew they were bent.

Barnwell was different. She'd no animus toward him. Indeed she knew nothing of him save that he was a fellow officer and had a good record. He was therefore someone she *wanted* to believe in. What was more, if she didn't believe in him, then the possibility she faced in his case was far worse than anything she'd faced with Tern or Hanlon. If it really was Barnwell who bled over that boy's body, then he wasn't merely a bent copper. He was probably a murderer.

And so she'd surely been just as stupid with him as Othello was with Iago. She'd simply assumed—no, *insisted*—that he couldn't be such a villain.

Until Michael put his questions.

But of course he could be such a villain and perhaps he was. And now that Michael's questions had been asked, she and her team must surely look again at everything in this case that involved DSI Barnwell.

Everything.

She sighed.

The clock in the sitting room chimed the half hour. Already the garden was full of morning light. She could hear Michael running the shower upstairs, and Figaro's paws clattering on the parquet. Any minute now she would hear voices from the children's bedroom.

She drank the rest of her coffee and stood up.

The day was beginning.

THIRTY-FIVE

Cecilia arrived at her office much preoccupied with her new thoughts. But she hardly had her coat off before the light was flashing on the phone on her desk.

She picked up. "DSI Cavaliere here."

"Tom Foss here, from your local friendly laboratory."

"Good morning Tom. So what's up?"

"You asked for a report on that rope," he said, "the one that was used to hang James Farthing."

"So I did." The truth was, she'd completely forgotten about it.

"Well," he said, "we got to it."

Which was a lot quicker than she'd have expected. "And?"

"And I'm sending you a write up, but I thought you'd like to know the main results straight away."

"And they are?" Dear Tom! He was good at what he did, and she was fond of him in an odd sort of way. But he did love to string things out.

"Well, there were several results on it that we don't recognize. No matches to anyone on the national database or anywhere else that we can access. Of course you'd expect that. All sorts of people could have handled the thing for all sorts of reasons over the last twenty years. But we do have two matches, and I think they'll interest you."

She waited.

"First, it was handled quite a lot by the same person that bled over the other boy's clothes."

"Was it, indeed?" That was a useful link. And given her new-found suspicions, would fit with the bleeder being Barnwell, since he'd certainly handled the rope. So far, so good. "And second?"

"And second, it was handled by one of the golf club members you took samples from the other day."

"That's interesting. And who was that?"

"Gregory Catesby."

"*Gregory Catesby!*" She frowned. "Are you sure?"

"We are. We imagine he perspired on it—pulling on it, maybe?"

"I see." She shook her head. Of all the possibilities, that was perhaps the last name she would have expected. "Well thank you very much, Tom—and your people. This could be really helpful."

"All part of the service!" he said. "The full report with all its gory and sweaty details—mostly sweaty, I'm afraid—is on your computer, or should be any minute now."

She thanked him again, asked him to copy the report to the other members of the Serious Crimes Team, and rang off.

She sat back, but only for a moment before picking up the phone again.

"Verity, I need you and the rest of the team in my office straight away. We have a lot to talk about."

"On it, ma'am."

THIRTY-SIX

Heavitree Police Station, Cecilia's office. A few minutes later.

Joseph arrived a few minutes before the others.

"Tell me," Cecilia said, "would it be difficult to get a National Health Service blood donor's card that said you had a different blood group from your actual blood group?"

He shrugged. "Difficult for most people—especially since the NHS established an electronic data base in 2015. You'd have to hack into their records, and then change whatever they had about you in your Summary Care Record. Most people wouldn't know how to do that. Of course it would also be a pretty silly thing to do, since it's rather in your interest that your SCR details be correct!"

"But it could be done?"

"I dare say MI6 would know how to do it. And the CIA."

"Would *you* know how to hack into the NHS data base?"

He gazed skywards. "I dare say I *might* manage it if I thought about it very hard. But then," he added in a tone of ostentatious virtue, "it would be very wrong of me!"

She smiled. "Right. Of course it would. But what about in 1994? Could you have got a card with the details changed back then?"

He stared at her for a moment, and then nodded. "So *that's* where you're going, is it?" He paused. "I don't know. Back then I don't think there'd have been anything to hack. It *might* have involved no more than saying you'd lost your old card, but you knew your blood group so could you please have a new one? I dare say a senior police officer like Barnwell might not have too much difficulty conning some junior NHS clerk into issuing it. After all, it's not as if it was something they were guarding against. Why would they expect any normal person to want to carry a card that gave the wrong information?"

Cecilia nodded. "That makes sense."

The others began coming into her office. As they were doing so, Joseph took out his mobile and texted something.

Cecilia began by filling them in on the main results of the lab report.

"It should be on your computers by the time you get back to your desks," she concluded, "but I understand that's the gist of it."

Verity shook her head at what she had heard. "Gregory Catesby! And he wasn't much more than a boy himself. He was seventeen, wasn't he?"

Cecilia shrugged. "Murders have been committed by ten-year-olds."

"And," Headley said, "Gregory Catesby was perhaps a very rich seventeen-year-old who was used to getting his own way."

Joseph laughed cynically. "And there is his legal defense. Affluenza!"

The others stared at him.

"What?" Verity said.

"Affluenza. It means you've grown up so rich and privileged you haven't had a chance to learn that actions have consequences or the difference between right and wrong."

"That's ridiculous!" Verity said.

"Ridiculous or not, a teenager in Texas who'd killed four people and injured nine others while driving drunk used it a couple of years ago—at least his lawyers did—and he got off with probation."

"There has to be more to it than that."

Joseph shrugged. "There is. It's what happens when you have a system where you choose judges for their political ideology rather than their commitment to interpreting the law, and you don't properly separate the judiciary from the executive."

"All this is fascinating," Cecilia said, "but could we get back to the point?"

"Well part of the point is surely this," Verity said. "The lab report does something beside tying Gregory Catesby to the second murder scene, or at least the murder weapon. It indirectly confirms what we already thought—that the first and second murders are connected. We now have Mr. X, whoever he was, involved in both of them—having his nosebleed all over young Kermode, and then also handling the rope that hanged Farthing."

"That's right," Cecilia said. "And we know of at least one man who was around at the time and who was suffering from nosebleeds, don't we?"

Verity frowned.

"Barnwell?" she said. "But his blood group wasn't right."

"And how do we know that?" Cecilia said.

"Because he—oh!" Verity, like her husband, of course grasped the whole argument in a moment. "Actually, we *don't* know, do we? We only know it's what he told DIs Wesson and Smith. And waved a donor card at them that they probably didn't even look at properly. Oh my God, why on earth didn't I see that sooner?"

"Exactly. Why didn't any of us? I think it's been staring at me for days, but it was Michael coming back at me last night that made me actually *see* it. We've been saying all through that Barnwell was careless, incompetent, suffering from burnout, whatever. But we need to consider the possibility that he wasn't being careless or suffering from burnout at all. We need to consider that maybe he was the killer."

The four looked at each other. Suddenly, various things began to fall into place.

"Which, of course, would explain why he didn't want anyone inspecting either crime scene too closely," Tom said.

Headley nodded. "But then he has his team spend hours of time meticulously questioning every one in the world from Alphington to Timbuktu, and checking their sets of golf clubs and God knows what else, because he knows perfectly well that none of that will lead anywhere."

"Except," Joseph said, "that according to DIs Smith and Wesson, there were two sets of golf clubs that he *did* check for himself—Farthing's and Catesby's. Which would be rather convenient if Catesby was also somehow involved."

"Well hang on," Verity said. "The lab report ties Catesby to the *second* murder scene—Farthing's death. It doesn't actually tie him to the first—to Kermode's."

"It ties him to the second *murder*," Tom said, changing Verity's emphasis, "and you yourself just pointed out that overall the lab report confirms what we already thought—that the two murders were connected. Even a similar MO. So Catesby's involvement in one would seem to me more likely than not to imply his involvement in the other."

Verity nodded slowly. "Yes. Not necessarily, but quite possibly. I think that's reasonable."

Joseph's mobile phone buzzed. He looked at it. "That was quick," he said.

The others stared at him.

"While you were all coming in just now I texted the boffins downstairs to talk to the NHS and see if they still have medical records for Barnwell. It turns out they do, including his blood group, so we can find out if he was telling Wesson and Smith the truth or not. Of course it's his personal data, so to see it we'll need a warrant." He paused and gave a faint smile. "That, of course, is if you want to see it *officially*."

Cecilia shook her head. "Don't even go there! Anyway, for this I'm sure we can get a warrant. I'll get onto the chief super about it."

She made a note. She rather thought Davies already had an appointment with the judge later that morning, so perhaps he could apply for the warrant then.

"So," Headley said, "let's speculate. If Barnwell's NHS record *were* to show he lied about his blood group, that would suggest he had something to hide, such as that for some reason we can't yet fathom he's beaten the Kermode boy to a pulp, but in the process managed to get his nose bleed blood all over the body, which he is smart enough to realize could be a dead giveaway."

"And then," Tom said, "for some reason young Catesby also gets involved. Is that what we're saying?"

"Wait a minute," Verity said. "We're assuming that if Barnwell and Catesby were both involved, Barnwell was the killer and Catesby somehow got involved. But how if it was the other way round? Suppose *Catesby* was the killer, and then *Barnwell* got involved, such as by helping him hide the body and delay its discovery, something he might think of as an experienced police officer — but then he goes and has that embarrassing nosebleed over it?"

"And Catesby's motive for killing?" Tom said.

She shook her head. "I don't know."

"Could it still be something to do with those exercise books?" Joseph said. "Dad's affair with the local hottie?"

Verity sighed. "We're back on that are we? I still think it's a bit of a stretch."

"Maybe not such a stretch for a seventeen-year-old as for a sophisticated man like the major," Headley said. "And remember — even the other day Catesby went on about there being nothing he wouldn't do to save the family honor."

"That's true," Cecilia said. "Somewhat over the top, I thought, even at the time."

"So then Barnwell's motive for helping Catesby rather than arresting him would be what?"

"We've already noticed Catesby is rich," Headley said. "So why not greed? Who said, 'When in doubt, follow the money'?"

"Deep Throat said it," Joseph said. "I don't think it's invariably true. People kill people for all sorts of weird reasons."

Cecilia nodded. Think of Othello!

"Still," Verity said, "greed's always worth considering."

"Regardless of theories about motives," Cecilia said, "we need *first* to find out Barnwell's blood group, and so to find out whether he was lying. Which should be easy enough. But *then* we have to catch up with him, which may not be easy at all, or even possible. The good news is, we don't have that problem with Gregory Catesby, and he's also got something to explain: his link to the rope that killed James Farthing. I'll check with Davies when I ask him about the warrant, but I'm pretty sure that we'd be justified at least in bringing him in for questioning over that."

THIRTY-SEVEN

An interview room at Heavitree Police Station. Later that day.

G regory Catesby, plump and cheerful in a Harris Tweed sports jacket, fawn cavalry twills and a yellow tie, presented himself for interview at 1:30 p.m., without a solicitor.

Headley, Tom, and Joseph were to watch through the one-way glass from outside the interview room. Sergeant Stillwell and a uniformed constable were on hand. Cecilia and Verity would conduct the interview.

Cecilia began by pointing out to Catesby that their conversation was being videoed, indicating as was her custom that this was as much a means of checking on the police as on the witness.

She continued formally, "Mr. Catesby, you are being interviewed under caution. Which is to say, you aren't under arrest, you aren't obliged to answer any of our questions, and you are free to go at any time. It may harm your defense, however, if you don't mention when we question you something that you later rely on in court, and anything you *do* say may be given in evidence. Do you understand this?"

Gregory Catesby appeared unfazed by this formality. "Of course," he said cheerfully.

Cecilia glanced at Verity sitting next to her, who nodded.

"I should also point out to you that while we question you, you are entitled to be accompanied by legal counsel."

He grinned. "I appreciate you're doing everything by the book, Detective Superintendent. But I trust the law and so far as I know I haven't done anything wrong. So I think I should be able to manage without a legal johnny! There is just one thing, though."

"Yes?"

"I hate to be a bother, but I do seem to have developed a raging thirst. Is there any chance I could have a glass of water?"

"Of course you could."

Cecilia nodded to the constable, who disappeared.

"Mr. Catesby," she continued, "we are investigating a murder. Until we have a solution, as you yourself pointed out to your colleagues at the club some days ago, everyone is a suspect."

"I know," he said, still cheerful, "but I still think I can speak for myself."

"All right. But if at any time in our conversation you change your mind and decide you *do* need a solicitor, all you need do is say so, and I'll stop the interview until someone can be present for you."

"If that happens, I'll be sure to let you know."

"Thank you."

The constable reappeared with a pitcher of water and a glass, and filled the glass for him. Catesby nodded his thanks to them and drank from the glass gratefully.

Cecilia meanwhile looked at her notes and then back at him. If he was guilty, then he was good. Indeed, he was very good. There was no doubt about that. He showed some signs of nerves—the thirst was surely part of that—but surely no more than was reasonable in a man who found himself in a police station being questioned about a murder. If it hadn't been for the DNA, she'd still have believed he was innocent. But evidence was evidence.

"About the boy who was murdered," she said. "As you know, we re-opened this investigation because of fresh evidence about the blood on his clothes."

Catesby very slightly raised his eyebrows.

He knows he's safe there. He isn't worried.

"But another thing we've now found out about young Frank Kermode is that he was in the habit of watching people in the village carefully, and then writing what he saw them doing in exercise books. I know you were only a young man at the time—you were seventeen, I think—but did you know about this habit of his?"

"I'm afraid I have no idea what you are talking about," he said.

But at her mention of the exercise books there had been a slight widening of his eyes, a momentary parting of his lips. And in any case, wasn't his answer just a shade too elaborate?

"I'm surprised," she said. "We've been asking around the village and all sorts of local people do seem to have known. Several of them remember."

"Well, now that you mention it, I may have heard."

Changing your story already? It might have been wiser to say you don't listen to local gossip. She began to feel a little more confident.

"Well," she said, "young Frankie was a very observant little boy. Made something of a hobby of it. And wrote down everything he saw. Those books are most informative, even twenty years later."

Again his eyes widened slightly. "And you still have them?" he said.

"Why wouldn't we have them?"

"I thought that—no—I've already told you. I have no idea what you are talking about."

"So you say, Mr. Catesby."

But you do know what I'm talking about and I'm pretty sure you thought they'd been destroyed.

She leaned forward. "There's actually quite a lot in there about your family. Well, to be exact I should say about your father and a Mrs. Fletcher. It looks as though he couldn't get enough of her."

"If that's in the books then the boy was just making things up."

"As I've already told you, we've been asking around the village — general inquiries — and it's what lots of folks who were around at the time say."

He shook his head. "Let me tell you once and for all, I have no idea or interest in whatever someone may have scraped up from listening to gossip. My father was an officer and a gentleman — "

"Oh yes, an *officer*, with a military record — that was a bit odd too, wasn't it? I see his regiment had been due to go to the Falklands in '82, and he got a sudden pulled muscle or a gammy leg or something and couldn't go. Very convenient!"

Catesby's relaxed manner vanished, and his expression grew cold. "Just what are you insinuating?"

"I'm not insinuating anything, Mr. Catesby. I'm just reciting the record. But doesn't it sound rather as though your father was an excellent soldier as long as there wasn't any actual fighting to be done?"

"You bitch!"

Leaping from his seat he lunged at Cecilia — to be stopped in mid-lunge as Sergeant Stillwell, moving with surprising speed for a man of his size, grasped him by his shoulders and pressed him gently but firmly back down onto the chair.

"Now then, sir!" he said calmly. "No need for us to get excited!"

"Thank you, Sergeant Stillwell!" Cecilia said. She sat back in her chair. "Why, Mr. Catesby, what a violent temper you have!

You could easily have struck me, plunging around like that. And then you'd have been in serious trouble. We don't like people who strike police officers, do we, Detective Inspector Jones?"

"We certainly don't, ma'am," Verity said. "But isn't he in serious trouble anyway?"

"Of course he is! Thank you for reminding me. Let's move on from Major Catesby. In fact let's move on from the murder of Frank Kermode to that other murder. Yes," — turning back to Catesby — "you see the thing is, and talking of murder, we now know James Farthing didn't commit suicide."

"He was stunned with a golf club," Verity said, "and *then* someone pulled him up by a rope and hanged him." Taking up the questioning, she leaned forward. "And we know who the someone was."

She sat back and stared at him.

"It was you," she said. "And Detective Superintendent Barnwell helped you cover it all up. Just like he did after you'd killed Kermode."

Since, as Verity herself had pointed out that morning, they'd no actual evidence connecting Catesby to the death of Kermode, that was a somewhat risky shot in the dark, but then —

"There is absolutely no way you could prove any of that," he said.

Cecilia and Verity exchanged glances and Cecilia shook her head.

"You know, Mr. Catesby, as a police officer I've found over the years that when I accuse somebody and they're innocent they say, 'I didn't do it!' or, 'That's not true!' or even, 'It wasn't like that!' But 'You can't prove it!' is what they say when they know they're guilty as hell only they think we haven't got anything on them. Isn't that right, Detective Inspector Jones?"

"It is indeed, ma'am."

It was time, Cecilia decided, to go for the jugular.

"Only the thing is," she said turning to Catesby, "in this particular case we *do* have something on you." She paused. "Mr. Catesby, I bet you have absolutely no idea how long DNA lasts, even on a piece of rope. Under some circumstances, about 6.5 million years! Isn't that right, Detective Inspector?"

"Well to be fair, ma'am," Verity said with that air of innocent helpfulness at which she was so good, "we should perhaps admit that it's probably not readable after about 1.5 million years."

"Very true, Detective Inspector. I was forgetting that. But then" — Cecilia turned back to Catesby — "we didn't have to deal with anything like that length of time in this case, did we, Mr. Catesby? It's just a little over twenty-one years since you pulled on that rope, isn't it? So that means we've got however many are left when you take twenty-one from 1.5 million years to spare. How many would that be, Detective Inspector?"

"That would be a lot," Verity said.

"There you are, Mr. Catesby: a lot. Detective Inspector Jones knows about these things. And what that boils down to is that at this point in time the DNA is still perfectly readable. It was *you* pulled on that rope, the rope that hanged James Farthing, the rope we still have in evidence, and therefore the rope that's going to convict you of murder."

Catesby scowled, and for a moment looked as if he might lunge again. Sergeant Stillwell, still standing by the door, gave a cough, shifted slightly on the balls of his feet, and flexed his fingers.

"If I were you," Cecilia said to Catesby, "I really wouldn't do it."

There was a pause. Then Catesby settled back in his chair, his scowl vanished, and abruptly, like sunshine breaking through cloud, his cheerful smile returned.

"You know, Detective Superintendent," he said, "if you don't mind and the offer's still open, I think perhaps I'll avail myself of that solicitor after all."

He might have been asking for a cup of tea.

Cecilia nodded. "Good idea, Mr. Catesby."

"And," he added, "it's one million, four hundred and ninety-nine thousand, nine hundred and seventy-nine."

"What is?"

"What's left when you take twenty-one from 1.5 million."

"Oh," she said. "Thank you."

"Don't mention it."

The golf club had not, it seemed, made him treasurer for no reason.

THIRTY-EIGHT

*The same interview room at Heavitree Police Station.
About an hour later.*

When Cecilia and Verity returned to the interview room, Catesby had a solicitor sitting beside him — a man Cecilia recognized. Roy Charles John Gillon, a local man with offices in the Cathedral Close. She respected him. He knew his job.

Cecilia nodded a greeting to him as she took her seat opposite, and he nodded back. She looked at her notes.

"All right, Mr. Catesby," she said. "Now that you know that we know you killed James Farthing, and we can pretty well prove it, let's start again, shall we?"

"Excuse me, Detective Superintendent," Gillon said, "I have no idea what you can possibly mean by saying that you can 'pretty well prove' that my client killed James Farthing. So far as I can see from my brief conference with Mr. Catesby just now, you have evidence that he at some point *touched the rope* that hanged this unfortunate young man. Presumably that could have been before or after his death? Incidentally, you say that James Farthing was *killed*, rather than committing suicide. You have evidence of that?"

"We do indeed, Mr. Gillon. The condition of the rope makes this perfectly clear."

"I see. You are saying that it is clear now, twenty years after the fact. And yet it was not clear to officers investigating on the scene at the time? Am I correct?"

"I'm afraid you are, Mr. Gillon."

"I see." Gillon nodded, and made a note.

"All right, Mr. Catesby," she said, "let us be more precise. We are now aware that James Farthing was killed by being hanged, rather than by his committing suicide, and the DNA evidence shows that you at some time handled the rope that hanged him. In short, you were in some way involved in his death."

"I think, Detective Superintendent," Gillon said, "that with your last observation you are again going rather beyond what the facts will show. Or at least your remarks, if unchallenged, could be interpreted as doing that. At the very least, I must point out that the phrase 'involved in' could mean many things, not all of them criminal or even culpable."

"That seems somewhat unlikely," Cecilia said.

"Not at all. Thus, for example, let me suggest to you that my client, then a teenage boy, walking innocently near to the golf course, simply *finds* the unfortunate young man hanging. He touches the rope, perhaps gives it a tug, as one well might—most likely thinking the scene is a practical joke, a schoolboy tease! But then he realizes that the young man is really dead! He panics and flees the scene! And then in his panic he does not admit to having been there at all! Very foolish of him, no doubt—indeed, reprehensible—but entirely understandable, and hardly grounds for accusing him of anything worse than teenage folly or cowardice. Surely if you are going to allege that my client has *killed* someone, you are intending to produce considerably more evidence than that?"

Gillon was good. There was no doubt about it. In a few sentences he had given a perfectly feasible alternative explanation of the evidence. She looked at Verity, who raised her eyebrows and gave a faint shrug. Suddenly the case against Catesby, which a couple of hours ago had looked convincing, seemed to be evaporating.

There was a tap at the door. She looked up, as a uniformed constable appeared.

"The chief super is here and would like a word, ma'am."

She suspended the interview for the purpose of the recording and followed the constable.

Glyn Davies was waiting for her. He looked sympathetic, but he shook his head. "I just watched the last bit of your interview. If it's any consolation to you, I think rather you're right. Catesby is guilty. But I'm also sure Gillon is right. You haven't got enough. You can't charge him. You'll have to let him go. That's the bad news."

She nodded. It was a bitter pill to swallow.

"But I also have good news," he said. "I saw the judge in his chambers just before lunch, and he gave us the search warrant. Joseph got straight on to the NHS with it, they've faxed us Barnwell's medical record, *and his blood group is O Rhd positive*, the same as the blood on Kermode's body. In other words, he lied about it, just as you suspected."

To be honest, she thought, just as Michael suspected.

"You've all been busy, sir," she said.

"That's not all of it. I've just had a teleconference with the Crown Prosecution Service — David Llewellyn, the local chap. You know him?"

She nodded. "Yes, sir."

"Well, a good man, and not inclined to be over confident. Anyway, in view of what we now have, he's quite clear there's *already* a viable prima facie case as accessory to murder against ex-Detective Superintendent Barnwell. None of us has much doubt that if we arrested him and took a DNA sample — which we'd be entitled to do if we'd arrested him — it would confirm that he was the person who moved Frank Kermode's body. And if we can get *him*, then very possibly he'll give us Catesby.

So—we keep on looking for Barnwell, and we don't give up hope of getting arrests and convictions out of all this. Only not today! Bad luck!"

She nodded. "Yes, sir."

This was better, but it was still jam tomorrow—probably. As far as today was concerned, she would not be enjoying the next five minutes.

She walked back to the interview room and looked down at Catesby, who was still seated with his lawyer behind the table, with Verity seated opposite them. She gritted her teeth.

"Thank you, Mr. Catesby," she said. "We've finished our questions for the time being. You are free to leave whenever you wish."

Catesby got to his feet at once. Gillon remained seated a moment longer, gathering his notes into his briefcase.

Catesby smiled pleasantly at Cecilia.

"Well," he said, "what an interesting afternoon! I do hope that you enjoyed it as half as much as I did!"

She smiled sweetly back. "Good afternoon, Mr. Catesby," she said.

THIRTY-NINE

Cecilia's office. Some minutes later.

"Disaster!" Verity said when the five team members met in Cecilia's office some minutes later.

They all looked crestfallen.

It dawned on Cecilia that at this moment it was her job to rally the troops, just as the chief superintendent had earlier rallied her.

"Not at all," she said, with a brightness that she did not entirely feel. "Catesby had good legal counsel—as was his right—and we lost a battle. That doesn't mean we've lost the war."

She went on, first, to make sure everyone was up to date with the latest developments in the case against ex-DSI Barnwell.

"The point is," she said, "if we get Barnwell, then he may give us Catesby. We have to be patient." She leaned forward. "Second: it's been a surprisingly quiet week but the world isn't standing still. Three things have come in today. Nothing huge or that we'll have a problem dealing with, but they all need our attention. So let's get to them first thing tomorrow morning. Put the 1994 business on hold for the moment. The new files are all on your computers. Verity, will you allocate tasks?"

"Yes ma'am."

Finally, she looked at Joseph. "And third, Joseph—despite what I've just said, I do want *you* to stay on Catesby. Here's the thing about that. If Catesby was the pitiless killer we think he was when he was seventeen, and got away with it, then I doubt very much he's been leading a life of sweetness and light ever since. Up until now we've been concentrating on what happened in 1994. I'd like to widen the net. What's he been up to since 1994? Since he left school? What are his connections? What does he do with himself when he's not being membership secretary and treasurer of Abingdon Golf and Country? Does he work? Does he play? Who with?"

Joseph grinned. "On it, ma'am! As they say, it ain't over till the fat lady sings."

"Well, no, not if you like that sort of thing," Cecilia said. "Personally I prefer Violetta to Brünnhilde any day, but there's no accounting for taste."

FORTY

Jenny was lying in the bed in her pink bedjacket and looking very fragile this morning, but she smiled up at Michael from the pillow as he told her all the news.

"I always knew my lad would never have done a thing like that," she said, "and now your missus and her mates have gone and found out the blokes that did it! After all these years!"

"Yes, Jenny, they have. At least, they're pretty sure they know who they are."

"She's clever *and* lovely, your missus."

"Yes, she is," Michael said. "That's what I think, too."

"Not like me," Jenny said reminiscently. "I was a looker all right, but I wasn't clever. Thick as two short planks, I was! Always bottom of the class at school! Drove the teachers barmy!"

"You underestimate yourself, Jenny. You were clever enough to go on believing in Jimmy, regardless of what everyone else said."

She shook her head. "That was something I just knew. I didn't have to be clever." She paused. "It's a bit like waiting for the birds to come. Sometimes there ain't even one, like I said. But then suddenly a whole load turns up, or some marvelous bird you've never seen before. You just have to believe they'll come when it's time for them to come, not expect anything in particular, and watch what's going on in front of you. Cleverness don't come into it."

Michael nodded. *This woman appears to know how to meditate,* he thought, *and she's probably never even heard the word.*

"I'm sorry I can't sit up to talk to you today," Jenny said. "I don't mean to be rude. It's just that I don't seem able to today."

"That's fine, Jenny. You just stay as comfortable as you can."

"You know, Father, I've only got a bit of time left. Maybe a week or two. Not more."

"I know, Jenny."

"Don't get me wrong, Father, I'm looking forward to it. I mean, if the Almighty is the Almighty, then death's the next big adventure, isn't it?"

Michael nodded. "Yes, Jenny, I think it is."

"And this life is pretty good, mostly, except where people muck it up for each other. And I've had some lovely bits, spite of everything. So just think what the next one must be! It'll be amazing!"

She paused.

"'Course I know it's not up to me to tell the Almighty what to do, but you know how sometimes you think of things you've said that you wish you hadn't said? And things you ought to have done for people and didn't, and now you wish you *had* done?"

"I think of things like that all the time."

"Well, 'course the Almighty knows I've already said sorry to Him. But it'll be nice if there's a chance to say sorry to them, won't it? Put things right, like. Still, I expect the Almighty's got it sorted. It'll be all right in the end."

Again Michael nodded. *All shall be well, and all manner of thing*

shall be well. So far as he could see, this woman needed no counsel from him or anyone else about dying. She was ready.

"There's just one thing, Father."

"What's that, Jenny?"

"I'd like—well, I was wondering whether you'd do my service for me, you know, when I'm gone. In St. Mary's Church,
not that nasty little chapel at the crem. I know I'm not proper
C of E and all that, so maybe I shouldn't really be asking, but if
you could—"

"It'll be my honour, Jenny."

"Everything you've got, Father? Lots of bowing and
scraping?"

"That's a promise, Jenny. It'll be a full Requiem Mass. All the
bowing and scraping in the world! Count on it!"

FORTY-ONE

The War Memorial in front of St. Mary's Church, Exeter.
Sunday, 8th November. 10:30 a.m.

So far as Cecilia could recall it had rained at some point every day last week. But now on Remembrance Sunday morning it was fine — breezy, to be sure, but with sunshine, too. As they stood by the war memorial in front of the church, bunches of cloud went scudding across the sky and Michael's surplice and scarf fluttered about him. The Union Flag above her cracked and strained on its halyard. Normally on Sundays and at greater festivals they flew the English flag, the cross of St. George, which was also, Michael said, the Church of England's flag, insofar as it had one. But on Remembrance Sunday he thought the United Kingdom flag more appropriate. So they were flying that, its red, white, and blue brave against the sky.

Chief Superintendent Glyn Davies was at the main city service in the Cathedral, together with the Chief Constable and the mayor and other dignitaries. But he had given approval for Cecilia and any members of her team who wished to attend the Remembrance service at St. Mary's instead, only making it a condition that they wore uniform, as they would have been expected to do had they attended the Cathedral. So she had pulled hers out of the wardrobe, checked that her superintendent's crowns were still on the epaulettes (she had sewn them on last year, and her sewing was hardly the best in the world), brushed and pressed it, and been relieved to find that it still fitted after a whole year.

Michael always chortled when he saw her in uniform. "It's very sexy," he said. "I could definitely fancy you in that!"

Which was nice—but not, presumably, the reason Glyn Davies wanted her to wear it.

Anyway, here they all were round the stone war memorial outside the church, the people gathering quietly as the rubric said they should. Nothing to be heard save the rustling of clothes, the movement of shoes on gravel, occasional gusts of wind, and here and there a whispered "excuse me" or "thank you" as people found their places. The local branch of the Royal British Legion (in some sense, surely, the stars of this particular show) was there in force, medals gleaming. So, too, a small group of serving Royal Marines from Lympstone (surely Mr. Oakley, one of the church wardens, himself a retired major of marines, had something to do with that?), together with Scouts and Guides and Sea Scouts and Cubs and Brownies and all manner of others, old and young, hale and sick, some in wheelchairs and some on crutches, all here to honour the fallen.

And, of course, there was her own little team: Verity in uniform with her inspector's "pips" ("Order of Bath Stars" to the initiated) on the epaulettes (Cecilia had passed them on to her when they were both promoted last year). Of course Verity looked stunning, as she always did. The dark blue and silver of police uniform went well with her blonde hair. But then, what didn't? Joseph was beside her, handsome as ever in his dark suit ("my beautiful Bahamian" Verity had whispered to her once). And beside them Headley and Tom, dapper and dutiful in uniform but looking, to tell the truth, somewhat ill at ease. They would probably have been happier with the main group of officers in the cathedral. They'd come to St. Mary's, she was sure, out of loyalty to the team and perhaps even out of loyalty to her, but neither was a churchgoer, and they did not, she imagined, feel very comfortable in the setting of a parish church. The relative anonymity of the main civic gathering would have suited them better.

At the center of it all was Michael, flanked by the assistant priest—retired Father Crane who'd been vicar of St. Olaf's in the city many years ago—and two lay readers. Beside them the choir, shuffling and clutching its music, the younger members inclined to giggle and glared at by the director when they did.

Michael was looking very Anglican today, vested for the remembrance office in what she'd learned since their marriage to call "scarf and hood," his service sheet in his hand, his expression just slightly anxious as (at least to her eyes) it always was on special occasions: which, in her opinion, he generally carried off very well—partly, no doubt, because matching his anxiety with action, he always took care in preparation, and partly because he had in any case something of a flair for good theatre.

The church clock chimed the half hour and the ritual began, Michael reading ancient sentences of faith and hope, his voice clear and strong, "God is our hope and strength; a very present help in trouble."

She was glad he used the older wording. She thought the modern versions flabby.

Her mobile phone vibrated for a moment, then stopped. What a time to choose! Well, there was nothing she could do about it now.

An old man from the Legion stood and recited words that over the years had become traditional at remembrance:

"They shall grow not old, as we that are left grow old;

"age shall not weary them, nor the years condemn."

One of the young marines replied,

"At the going down of the sun and in the morning,

"we will remember them."

Everyone answered, "We will remember them."

A bugler stepped forward from the marines, and played the Last Post.

He played beautifully—the B♭ version, which she preferred—and it broke her heart, as it always did.

And now the two minutes' silence.

Heads bowed, weapons reversed, banners lowered.

The Union Flag snapping on its halyard.

Michael's surplice, moving in the wind.

Some of the children restless.

In the next street the sound of a window closing.

She thought of her uncle Andrea, the Carabiniere cadet who died in the battle for Rome.

The young German soldier killed at the Normandy beachhead, and the British soldier who'd exchanged fire with him weeping over his body, and still weeping fifty years later.

Julie Danvers, killed while saving a wounded comrade.

It was like every damned war, a waste of good men…

> But if the cause be not good, the king himself hath a heavy reckoning to make, when all those legs and arms and heads, chopped off in battle, shall join together at the latter day and cry all "We died at such a place."

But then, people died uselessly in peacetime, too.

Frank Kermode…

James Farthing…

Reveille startled her out of her thoughts—as, of course, it was meant to.

They said the Lord's Prayer. They sang "O God, our help in ages past." Someone read something from the Sermon on the Mount. And now they were laying wreaths and lighting candles. Verity jogged her gently, reminding her that she too, as senior officer present, had to lay a wreath on behalf of the police.

As she walked toward the stone cross a familiar five-year-old voice came from among the little ones and said, "Ooh, that's Mummy!" For a moment she smiled and others did too.

She took a breath and focused and did what was proper: laying the wreath, then stepping back two paces, coming smartly to attention and saluting, British army style, open palm facing forward, fingers almost but not quite touching her head-gear, long way up and short way down, exactly as Glyn Davies had personally taught her to do it, indeed, exactly as he had insisted she *must* do it — regardless of whatever "I-seem-to-have-lost-my-sunglasses nonsense" (his words) she might have seen among police officers from other forces.

"It's what Sergeant Wyatt would expect," he told her.

He knew her well. He could not have chosen an argument more likely to persuade her.

When they had finished these memorials, Mr. Oakley said the Kohima Epitaph:

"When you go home tell them of us and say,

"for your tomorrow we gave our today."

There were more prayers. They sang *God Save the Queen*. And Michael brought the office to an end, invoking grace for the living; rest for the departed; unity, peace, and concord for church, queen, commonwealth and humankind; and the bless-ing of the triune God upon them all.

"Amen," she said with everyone else and dutifully crossed herself.

Moving slowly with the rest of the congregation toward the church, she took a moment to peer at her mobile phone. There was a long text from Chief Superintendent Davies' office.

She stopped to read it, shadowing the phone with her hand against the sunlight.

They had finally located ex-Detective Superintendent

Timothy Barnwell. The retired police officer had migrated to Spain and changed his name twice, so it was no wonder they'd had trouble finding him. It was actually by way of his NHS records — those very records that Joseph had pointed them to — and requests from Spain for details of his medical history, that they had finally located him. He was now in hospital in Málaga, suffering from an inoperable cancer. The doctors reckoned he had at most weeks to live.

As a consequence of all this, she and Detective Inspector Verity Jones were booked on Flybe Flight 533 departing Exeter Airport at 10:25 a.m. tomorrow for Glasgow, then onward via London (why on earth were they going from Exeter to London *via Glasgow?*) to arrive in Málaga at 7:50 p.m. On their arrival at Málaga, Spanish police would meet them and see to their accommodations. On the following day they were to meet with Spanish legal authorities, and they should be able to interview ex-Detective Superintendent Timothy Barnwell in hospital on the day after that.

They would be carrying with them a warrant for his arrest.

FORTY-TWO

Málaga. Tuesday, 10th November 2015.

The time in Spain went by for Cecilia in something of a whirlwind, sometimes feeling like work, but at others, if truth be told, like being on holiday.

For the formalization of arrangements already agreed on informally between the Málaga police and the Devon and Cornwall constabulary, it was necessary that they present themselves before a Spanish judge. The basic plan was simple. Technically and legally, Barnwell was to be under arrest by the Devon and Cornwall Police and in custody, awaiting trial. In view of his health and apparently terminal condition he would, however, be allowed to remain where he was, under the physical custody of the Spanish authorities, until he died. If by any chance he recovered that would of course create a new situation and arrangements would have to be made for his extradition to England to stand trial. In view of the doctors' prognoses, no one expected that to happen.

That the basic plan was simple did not mean, however, that it did not involve several hours of signing documents and making depositions. It did not help, of course, that everything had to be done in two languages and with the help of an interpreter.

Cecilia's own Spanish was not particularly good, and Verity's was, as Verity herself admitted, "fluent enough to be dangerous," — being particularly characterized by an atrocious accent, and by its habit of devolving into Latin at crucial moments, to the manifest amusement of their Spanish colleagues. This latter characteristic was, of course, a consequence of her education, which had included a double first in *litterae humaniores* at Oxford — an experience from which, as Joseph occasionally pointed out, she had never entirely recovered.

It then transpired, however, that the elderly judge was also a fluent Latinist, and delighted to find someone with whom he could converse in his favorite language. After which it seemed that the services of an interpreter were hardly needed, and they all got on like a house on fire. The elderly judge did, indeed, seem vastly taken with Verity, and to Cecilia's amusement appeared toward the end of the proceedings to be addressing his remarks almost exclusively to her. It was, she believed, the first time she had ever watched anyone flirt in the language of Cicero. Even so, by the time all was completed and they went to lunch, she felt more exhausted than she usually did after a full day's work.

Then, since they were not to see Barnwell until the following morning, they had the afternoon free. This, of course, was the holiday part. The weather was glorious after the rain and murk of an Exeter November, and they were happy to spend some of their free time simply drinking coffee and looking at the Mediterranean. But they also dutifully visited some of city's sights — of which, given that it had at various periods been Phoenician, Carthaginian, Roman, Turkish, and Spanish, there were not a few. At Michael's special request, they even visited the Anglican cemetery — a cemetery surely being, as Verity pointed out, a not unsuitable place to by peered at by detectives on a murder inquiry.

"Who knows," she said, "what ancient crimes one might discover and investigate amid these stone angels and lichen-covered crosses?"

FORTY-THREE

St. Mary's Rectory, Exeter. About the same time.

"Daddy, daddy, Figaro and Tocco and Pu are fighting with Hoover in the garden!" Rachel called out. "They're hurting her!"

"I'm coming, sweetheart."

Moments later, Michael emerged from his study and came down the stairs, his head full, if truth be known, of what he and the prophet Malachi — *malāki, my messenger!* — should say to each other and the congregation on the following Sunday.

There was indeed a great deal of noise coming from the garden: growls and barks and yelps and scuffles and general doggy uproar.

He gazed out of the French windows to see three dogs and a puppy hurtling around the lawn and in and out of the shrubs that skirted it at breakneck speed. All four tails were wagging furiously. As they passed by, the occasional small bird rose into the air, tweeting irritably at the disturbance. A startled rabbit shot out of the bushes and scampered away into the hedge.

The basic ritual was that Hoover would hurl herself at one of the older dogs, and in turn be hurled back onto the grassy ground, where she would tumble over and over until finding her feet again and at once flinging herself back into the fray — an exercise endlessly repeated that clearly afforded both her and her companions immense satisfaction.

Michael watched admiring for a minute or so.

How utterly in the moment they were!

How transported, how lost to themselves in the joy of being, and of being together!

Then he looked at Rachel and shook his head. "No, sweetheart, they're not hurting her. They're fine. And Hoover is having a lovely time. Figaro and Tocco and Pu are teaching her how to be a dog. And incidentally, they're also making her part of the pack."

"Oh." Rachel sounded, if anything, disappointed. "I thought," she added with just a hint of sulkiness, "Hoover might want to come and play with me."

"I think just at the moment she'd rather be with the others. I expect she'll want to come to you for a cuddle later."

"Oh."

He sighed. Poor Rachel! Another hard lesson to be learned in life! We do so love our doggies, and for the most part they are surely quite fond of us. So what a cruel blow to our egos it is to realize that sometimes, nonetheless, they actually prefer the company of other dogs!

FORTY-FOUR

Málaga, Spain. That evening.

In the evening, Cecilia and Verity's Spanish colleagues took responsibility for their feeding and entertainment. It was obvious that a group of them—mostly young men—had been told some days ago to spend the evening keeping the two visiting British police officers happy. It was equally obvious that Cecilia and Verity were not at all what they had been expecting, and that they were delighted by the surprise. The evening was uncomplicatedly pleasant and, as Verity remarked when they arrived back at their hotel, it was remarkable how her Spanish seemed to improve after a few glasses of *tinto de verano*.

Cecilia agreed but, as she told Michael when she telephoned him from her bed before going to sleep, she had no explanation for this remarkable phenomenon.

Neither had he, but after listening gravely to her narrative, he did have a possible alternative description of it.

"Could it be," he said, "that you and your Spanish friends are all getting better at understanding Verity's Latin?"

This, she admitted to herself some time later as she drifted into oblivion, was an idea that had not previously occurred to her.

But it certainly merited consideration.

FORTY-FIVE

Málaga. Verity's hotel room, the following morning.

After good coffee and croissants in the hotel restaurant, Cecilia and Verity gathered in Verity's room. Joseph had said that he would come through to them on Verity's iPad at 8:15 a.m.—9:15 a.m. in Exeter—and he was on time to the minute. Just, of course, as Cecilia expected.

They exchanged pleasantries about the weather, glorious in Málaga, raining again in Exeter; about Hoover, who (possibly stimulated by her adventures in learning to be a dog) had last night mistaken a copy of Alan Bennett's *Six Poets: Hardy to Larkin* for a bone and chewed the corner off ("but you can still read most of it perfectly well," Joseph said, "all except an inch or two off the top of the introduction, and you can generally guess what he's saying there"); and about the infant Samuel, who was missing his mother but being compensated by spending his days at the rectory with Hoover and being thoroughly spoiled by Cecilia's mama.

Despite my love for the land of my forbears and all things Italian, Cecilia wondered, does it show how British I have become that I see nothing odd in the fact that my dear friends, obviously caring and devoted parents as they are, nonetheless talk to each other first about the weather, then about their dog, and only afterwards about their child?

These pleasantries completed, Joseph came to the point: which was Gregory Catesby.

"You asked me to investigate him," he said, "and I've spent the best part of the last two days on it. I've talked to people that know him. I've checked his flat—he lives in a small apartment in the golf club—his bank records, his files at the club, and everything on his computer. And before you ask, yes, I had a warrant. 'Reason to believe' et cetera et cetera. Chief Superintendent Davies fixed all up that for me."

Cecilia nodded.

"I've also sent his fingerprints and the record of his DNA to Interpol, Europol, and the FBI."

"His fingerprints? How did we come to have those?"

"I'd saved the glass he drank from in the interview room when you interviewed him. In case it came in handy."

She smiled. Joseph seldom missed a trick. "That's excellent," she said. "Terrific work, Joseph!"

"I thought you'd like that part," he said. "Well, every silver lining has a cloud, and here's the part you won't like. I haven't come up with a damn thing. Nobody in crime fighting has ever heard of him. None of his details match anything on anyone's databases. So far as the records show, Gregory Catesby is squeaky clean and has been a model citizen all his life."

"Oh."

"And that's not the half of it. He's wealthy, of course. He has old money, and plenty of it, so he doesn't actually *need* to do anything. But in fact he does a lot. His being membership secretary and treasurer of the golf club naturally takes up quite a bit of time. But besides that he's a big supporter of Save the Children. And not just with money. He's down on the ground with the volunteers. Every Friday he's in the shop in Paris Street, serving. The local secretary says she reckons he's the best salesperson they've got. And do you remember the big concert they put on for Save the Children last year, the one Princess Anne attended?"

"I do." Cecilia had attended it herself, with Michael and Mama and Papa. It had been mostly Gilbert and Sullivan, which was not perhaps her favorite music in the world, but still the evening had been fun.

"Well, Gregory Catesby was pretty well the organizing genius behind that whole thing. He put hours into it—booking the orchestra, the singers, the venue, publicity, the lot. Weeks of work! And he did it all for absolutely nothing—well, he got presented to HRH, I think. That was his pay for a month's work! Twenty seconds of being chatted up by a royal!" He paused. "And then again," he said, "there's the Blue Sovereign."

"Really? What does he do for them?"

The Blue Sovereign was a residential recovery home near Exeter where children and their mothers could recover from abuse and dysfunction. Michael was an ardent supporter.

"He gives them money. They're all right financially now, but there were a couple of years early on when according to the woman who runs the place they couldn't have got by without his donations—and I mean *serious* money."

"Hmm."

"And before you start thinking nasty thoughts about vulnerable young women and children at risk—as far as Gregory Catesby and The Blue Sovereign is concerned, forget it. He's given them money, and *only* money. So far as I can learn, he's never even set foot in the place. The woman that runs it says she doesn't think he even knows where it is. All she knows is, every time they were in a financial jam and she let him know, she received a fat donation by return post that solved the problem."

Cecilia nodded.

"The last major contact I've got," Joseph said, "is that he goes quite a lot to the Benedictine house at Shillingford Abbot—St.

Loye's House. He goes there regularly to Mass on Sundays with the fathers, and is generally a friend of the place. I talked to a couple of the monks and they think very highly of him. He's a Catholic, of course. The family always has been, right back to the Reformation."

Cecilia nodded. She was well aware of St. Loye's at Shillingford Abbot. It was an offshoot of the Benedictines at Buckfast, a small residential house specifically devoted to treating addiction. Several of the monks were qualified therapists. Michael had sent a couple of parishioners there for help at various times, and one of the monks was a friend of his.

"Finally," Joseph said, "in addition to all these good works, everyone I've talked to that has to deal with Catesby on a personal level — servants at the golf club, the steward, people in the local shops, the pub — they all seem simply to *like* the man. They say he's funny, nice, always has a kind word for everyone."

And that, Cecilia reflected, was exactly the effect he had on me when I first met him.

"And you don't think there's any way this could somehow be a scam?" she said. "Are we being bamboozled?"

"I don't think so," Joseph said. "Too many different sources of information all say the same thing! Whether we like it or not, I think what you might call the 'good' part of Gregory Catesby is for real."

"Damn!" Cecilia said. How much simpler life was when villains were content simply to be villains!

"If we didn't know about his DNA being on the rope that hanged James Farthing," Joseph continued, "I'd probably say the man was in a quiet way something of saint. As it is, I don't know what to think of him. He's 'a riddle wrapped in a mystery inside an enigma.'"

That was certainly one way of putting it.

There was a pause.

"His middle name, by the way, is Eric," Joseph said.

"Is it now?" Cecilia said. "With a *c* or a *k*?"

"A *c*."

"Then that settles it," she said. "Of course he'll be a good person. We should have known."

Joseph looked puzzled. "We should? Why?"

Verity giggled.

Cecilia shook her head. "Joseph, you obviously haven't read the right kind of books. Erik with a *k* is always evil and malignant. Eric with a *c* is good and kind. Isn't that so, Verity?"

"Anybody knows that," Verity said.

"Or at least," Cecilia said, "anybody who knows anything about anything."

Forty-Six

Málaga. Hospiten Estepona.
A little after 10:00 a.m. the same day.

"Oh, I say, *very* smooth!" Verity said as their car drew up at the entrance to the Estepona Hospital.

It was indeed. The building that lay in bright sunlight before them, only meters from the Carretera Nacional 340, was sleek and elegant, with extensive lawns dotted with trees in front of it, and the heights of the Sierra Bermeja looming dramatically behind it.

"I gather that if you have to be ill in southwestern Spain, this is the place to be," Cecilia said. "It's only about ten years old and it's got some of the best equipment and staff in Europe. I also gather it's very pricey."

The uniformed Spanish officer who had brought them—in fact, one of their new friends from the previous evening—emerged from other side of the car carrying recording equipment. He gestured cheerfully at the Hospiten Estepona as if he had somehow created it for them himself, and grinned.

"Todo nos espera, señoras detectives," he said. "¡Síganme!"

They followed obediently.

The doctor who appeared a few minutes after they had presented themselves and their credentials at the reception desk was Spanish, but he spoke excellent English.

"There is little we can do other than keep the poor fellow comfortable," he said as they walked together through the hospital. "His cancer is, alas, inoperable."

"How long do you think he has?" Cecilia asked.

The doctor shook his head. "It's hard to say. I imagine he has a couple of months at most, but by the same token he may take a sudden turn for the worse, and then it could be no more than days. Here he is."

They entered a well-appointed private ward. A nurse, who had been tidying the room, stepped aside, and, at a sign from the doctor, waited quietly.

The photographs Cecilia and Verity had seen previously of DSI Timothy Barnwell were of a man stocky and solid. The Timothy Barnwell in a hospital bed who now gazed up at them was gaunt and pale, a fading shadow of his former self.

"You are ex-Detective Superintendent Timothy Barnwell, formerly of Exeter CID?" Cecilia said.

"Who wants to know?" His voice was weak and rasping.

"I am Detective Superintendent Cavaliere of Exeter CID, and this is Detective Inspector Jones, also of Exeter CID. We are here, as you see, with the permission and assistance of the Spanish authorities for law enforcement. This is Agente González of the Cuerpo Nacional de Policía."

"And so?" Barnwell said.

"Timothy Barnwell, I am arresting you as an accessory to the murder of Frank Kermode on the first of September 1994, and of James Farthing on the fifth of September 1994, and for conspiracy to pervert the course of justice. You do not have to say anything but it may harm your defense if you do not mention when questioned something which you later rely on in court. Anything you do say may be given in evidence."

"Well," he said, "it took you all long enough!"

FORTY-SEVEN

Hospiten Estepona. Timothy Barnwell's room.
Moments later.

"And I don't mind telling you," Barnwell said, "the new form of caution is a wordy pile of crap compared with the old."

Cecilia allowed herself the ghost of a smile. "I think it's a bit of a mouthful myself. But there you are, it is what it is."

There were several chairs in the room, so she sat down by the bed and indicated that Verity and Agente González should do the same.

"All right," Barnwell said, "so you've done it. Bully for you, though I don't know what you expect to achieve by it. The doctors tell me I'm inoperable. There's nothing they can do. I've got a couple of months at most. I'll probably be dead before you can even get me back to England, let alone into court."

"We know that," Cecilia said, "and you are to remain here, without any change of regimen for the duration of your illness. I want to make that clear. But you are formally under arrest, and we do wish to interview you, and to record the interview. It may also be, if you are still well enough, that you'll be asked to testify from here by satellite at a trial to be conducted in England. Of course you're entitled to have legal counsel with you on all such occasions, including now, and we can arrange that for you."

He smiled weakly. "For God's sake woman, don't you hear me? I'm a dead man. It's all one now. If I can tell you anything that will do anyone any good, they're welcome to it. What is it you want to know?"

Cecilia nodded. She turned to Agente González.

"¿Puede prender el equipo de grabación, por favor?" she said.

"Sí, detective superintendente."

As she had asked, he turned on the portable equipment. After a few seconds the tiny green light of the webcam came on. In the screen, small but clear, she could see the figures of Chief Superintendent Glyn Davies, Joseph, and—somewhat her surprise—a lanky figure whom after a few seconds of uncertainty she recognized as Sir Marcus Snowball, he of the paperback novel and the decadent Victoria sponge. She guessed that the chief superintendent, or perhaps even the Crown Prosecution Service, had decided that participation by a magistrate, even one "semi-retired," would lend more authority to the recorded interview if ever it had to be used as part of evidence in a legal proceeding.

Agente González made an adjustment that slightly brightened the screen, and another adjustment to the sound, and nodded to her.

"Gracias, agente," she said.

For the recording she identified the time and date, those participating, and the situation. She turned back to Barnwell and repeated her cautions. Finally, she came to questions.

"Our first question is what exactly happened on the day when Gregory Catesby killed Frank Kermode? We already know quite a lot, or I wouldn't be here, and of course we can make our guesses, especially after seeing your villa down the road. Swimming pool and all! Very elegant! But join up the dots for us."

He gave a slight shrug. "Why not? There was hardly anybody about on the course that day. I was playing a solitary round, just for practice. Of course I knew young Catesby had gone out ahead of me — his name was there in the book — and I was keeping a weather eye out for him, as one does. He wasn't very good, tended to lose balls and be very slow, and he had a massive handicap — I'm not sure how much, but pretty laughable. So there was always a chance I'd catch up with him. He wasn't at all like his father, incidentally, who could probably have been a pro if he'd wanted to be. In fact, his father used to laugh at him — quite openly, as I remember. To tell the truth, it wasn't very nice."

Cecilia raised an eyebrow.

"Anyway," he continued, "at the tenth, I came across young Catesby's stuff on the green, just standing there — his set of clubs and so on — but no sign of him at all. It was weird. I looked around for a bit and called out, and then I walked into the woods by the course, wondering if perhaps he'd gone in to look for a ball or something. But then, there he was — I nearly fell over him — standing by the body of the Kermode boy. And I mean *body. Corpse.* I could see straight away the kid was dead. Like a broken doll. Someone must have gone completely berserk. And there was Catesby looking down at him. I think I must have said, "What the hell happened to *him*?" or something like that, and he looked up at me, and he had a really strange expression on his face. And then he started to go on about it. 'The little squirt was going to blacken my father's name,' he said. 'He deserved what he got.' Funny little la-di-da accent he'd got. I can hear him now! I suppose it's what they taught him at that posh school he went to. Anyway, it was then I realized he'd actually killed the kid himself! For God's sake — I could see blood on the club he was holding! He babbled on and I gradually put together what had happened. The dead boy must have found out about the affair his father was having with that Fletcher woman in the village, written all the dates down in his little exercise books and then threatened Catesby he was going to tell the world about it. In fact lots of people knew about it anyway, including me, and frankly, I couldn't see why anyone would give a damn. But young Catesby was obsessed with family honour, or some such thing, and he'd completely lost it. I got the impression the Kermode boy teased him about it, jeered at him, and that caused young Catesby to go completely crazy. He grabbed a club, chased him into the wood, found him by the lane, knocked him unconscious, dragged him into the wooded area, and then beat him to a pulp. 'Creepy little prole got what he deserved!' he kept saying."

"So when did you decide to cover for him?"

"I suppose it sort of came to me gradually. I asked him, 'What do you think is going to happen to your great family name when this comes out?' and he obviously hadn't a clue. It was as if he thought that because they were Catesbys, every-one who was against them could be eliminated and that would be all right. And then I think it came to me: whatever I did, I couldn't bring back the dead. But perhaps young Kermode's death could be *my* big chance? Everyone knew the Catesbys were richer than God. How about a share in that for me?"

He paused, and Cecilia waited.

"Well—to cut a long story short, and I'm not sure I remem-ber all the details—I shoved young Catesby out of the way and took over. Clearly, the longer before the corpse was found the better it would be for him, so I dragged it over to a sort of ditch they were making and chucked it in and covered it with sticks and leaves."

"Just like that?"

"That's right."

"And no problems or anything while you were doing it?"

"I don't think—oh, wait a minute! I see what you're getting at. I had a bit of a nosebleed over the corpse while I was dragging it?"

Cecilia nodded. "Did that bother you?"

"Well," he said, "in those days we didn't do DNA, only blood groups, so I wasn't bothered about the blood itself. My blood group is the commonest in the UK anyway, so no one was going to identify me from that. But I was having a lot of nosebleeds about that time and people had noticed. I was worried forensics would work out that the blood spatter was from a nose bleed—as in fact they did—and that would make someone see a connection to me."

Cecilia nodded. "So what did you do?"

"I decided to create a back story. That evening in the pub—which was before anyone had even found the body or knew there was a murder, I made a big deal about my blood group being *A* Rhd positive. We'd had a blood drive the week before, so I was able to bring the subject up naturally enough. Even made a joke about how if they were O Rhd positive, their blood would be just fine for me if I needed some, but mine would kill them!"

"DIs Wesson and Smith said you showed them a donor card," Cecilia said. "How did you manage that? Did you somehow make one, or get it faked?"

He shook his head. "You overestimate my technical skills. I just used a trick I learnt years ago from an old con artist—a 'grifter,' I think, is the current term. I waved my real card at them for a second or two and *told* them it said I was A Rhd positive—and of course that was only one letter different from what it actually *did* say. It's amazing how if you show people something and tell them what they're seeing, provided they've no reason to distrust you and you don't go too far off the map, they'll believe you!"

Cecilia nodded. "I see. I did wonder about that." She paused. "So you got the corpse covered. Then what?"

"The next thing was I took Catesby's golf iron from him. Even at this point I don't think he really grasped the trouble he was in. He went on and on at me about the club being part of a 'damned expensive set,' as I dare say it was, and it being 'a bloody cheek' me asking for it. 'Yes,' I said, 'and it's also got your victim's blood and hair all over it, and I dare say your finger prints. It's a smoking gun, you idiot!' Christ, that boy was such a bloody fool! Well, we got things more or less sorted, and then I insisted we go back to the club together. I wasn't letting him out of my sight until I'd seen his parents, in case he did something else stupid."

Cecilia raised an eyebrow at Verity, who nodded: this corresponded more or less exactly to what the aged but evidently sharp and observant Glossop remembered seeing.

"After that," Barnwell said, "I insisted we go to his home. His mother and father were both there. His father had just got back from Scotland. He'd been at a meeting at the R & A. They were obviously taken aback to see us together, although of course I knew his father a bit from the club. Anyway, I didn't beat about the bush. 'I need to talk with you both,' I said, 'and while I do that, this boy of yours needs to take a bath and get every stitch of clothing he's wearing into the washer.' Somehow his father seemed to get the message. He looked at me, then at the boy, and then said, 'Do it!' So the boy suddenly grew completely meek and mild and went off and I dare say he did as he'd been told."

There was a pause.

"And then?" Cecilia prompted.

Barnwell took a breath. "Obviously, I'd got them dead to rights. They were so set on name and reputation! Well, *he* was set on it—the Major, as he insisted we call him. You know, I think Mrs. Catesby—Judy, her name was, she was a nice little thing—I think she really *didn't* realize her old man was knocking off the Fletcher bird. As I said, everyone else knew about it — in the golf club, in the village. It was common gossip. Everyone except her! Talk about love being blind. Anyway, I think the truth about that rattled her almost as much as finding out that their lad was a killer. But then there was the Major—'Daddy' as she kept calling him."

He stopped for a moment, recovering his breath, and then continued.

"God, there was a man full of shit if ever I saw one! He wasn't concerned about anything, so far as I could see, except, 'we've got to keep the family out of the papers.' The Catesby name was not to be smirched! Which of course meant *he* was not to be smirched. When I listened to him, I could see where his son had learnt all that crap about being a Catesby making you equal to God. And of course I was happy to go along with it for a price. The price, I told them, was half a million. That was reasonable. I was taking a hell of a risk."

"And they paid?"

"I'll say this for him, Catesby was as good as his word. Paid the money into a Swiss account for me the next day."

"And then?"

"And then, of course, all I had to do was make sure the investigation ran into the sand, which it was bound to since I was in charge of it and made damned sure it did."

Glyn Davies's grunt of irritation was audible from several hundred miles away. Cecilia glanced at the screen and then back again.

"And of course," she said, "you had no intention of questioning the person you knew had actually done it, or letting anyone else question him?"

"That's right. Him being not much more than a boy helped with that. Who would suspect that fine young Etonian of being a murderer?"

Cecilia nodded.

"And what about your claiming that James Farthing was a suspect?" Sir Marcus said suddenly from the screen. "How did that come about?"

"That was all a part of it. Of course Farthing's blood group being the same as mine and therefore the same as that on the victim was a bit of luck. I couldn't have banked on that! And another bit of luck was that when he was questioned he didn't have a proper alibi. But of course I knew none of it would really fly if it came to court. It was just smoke and mirrors—but it made a good show for the TV and the papers before I let him go. It showed everyone how hard we were working."

Sir Marcus nodded. "Yes, I can see that it would do that. As it happened it also put a vulnerable teenage boy under cruel pressure. But I dare say you were not much concerned about that." He paused for a moment, and then said, "Go on with your story."

Barnwell lay back for a few minutes and took deep breaths. Then he continued.

"In a few more days, the media would have lost interest and the whole thing petered out. The murder would have been put down to hooligans from the lane who'd picked up a driver from somewhere and got carried away with some violent game and then scarpered. And that would have been the end of it. James Farthing would have got over his little trauma and been fine. That was what I intended. Everything was under control. But then the arsehole Catesby has to be clever. Goes and *kills* James Farthing and tries to make it look like suicide. The silly little bugger hadn't a clue. When they found Farthing's body, of course they called me about the 'suicide'—as it happened I was already up at the clubhouse anyway. I went down there, took one look, and could see immediately that it was faked. Someone had stunned the lad and then strung him up to make it *look* like suicide. And of course I knew damned well who the someone must be."

"Even we could see the suicide was faked, just from the photographs, twenty years later," Verity said.

"I expect you could. The bloody photographer took those while I was tied up with something else, before I could stop him. And he was just about to go in and take close-ups. Christ, that would have torn it! Even I couldn't have covered that up. I tell you, I was tempted to let Catesby stew in his juice. But then of course I knew I couldn't do that. Apart from anything else, I was too involved myself."

Cecilia nodded. The *Macbeth* dilemma.

> *I am in blood*
>
> *Stepped in so far that should I wade no more,*
>
> *Returning were as tedious as go o'er.*

Barnwell lay back for a few minutes on the pillow and closed his eyes. He lay still for so long that for a moment Cecilia wondered if they had lost him. She looked at the nurse, who frowned, and seemed about to intervene. But then Barnwell himself looked up at them and continued, his voice now weaker.

"The upside was, I now had the family more than ever over a barrel. If I went down, they were sure as hell going down with me. So that evening, when they were all at home, I went round again. I think young Greg must have seen my car arrive. At any rate, he met me at the gate. Do you know, the idiot actually thought he'd got away with it? 'Well,' he says, 'it looks as if your suspect has admitted his guilt after all. Fancy him killing himself! Who on earth would have expected that?' I soon cleared him of that little delusion. 'Boy,' I told him, 'you're not only a bloody maniac — you're a bloody fool. I'll have to talk to your parents again.' And I tell you now, I made damn sure he walked *in front of me* up to the house. I was keeping that lethal little sod where I could see him. When I got there I told them that thanks to their son's stupidity the price had now gone up. It would be an extra two million. Daddy was like a punctured balloon. Mummy just sat silent. I don't think she spoke once while I was there. But Daddy would obviously do anything to stop his life being interfered with. So I got my two million, went along with the 'Farthing's suicide-was-an-admission-of-guilt' story, and generally got the thing wrapped up. Frankly, no one wanted a big fuss — the Alphington club had some important people in it — and if anything I got kudos for putting the thing to bed without too much fallout, rather then being questioned as to whether I'd really got at the truth."

Cecilia nodded. "We rather gathered that when we looked at the file."

"What happened to the golf club — the one Catesby used to kill James Farthing?" Sir Marcus asked. "I take it he must have used a second one, since you'd already got the first."

Barnwell frowned for a minute, then seemed to recollect. "I got the family to give it to me. Later of course I made a big show of the murder investigation team checking everyone's clubs, making sure that I did Catesby's myself, and of course I said they were all present and correct."

"So what did happen to them?" Sir Marcus pressed him. "Do you still have them?"

"The two clubs? I kept them until I could dispose of them safely. Now they're at the bottom of the Med."

Sir Marcus nodded. "I feared that might be the case."

"What happened to the exercise books?" Verity asked. "The ones Frank Kermode wrote all his stuff down in?"

"The parents said they didn't want them back so I chucked them."

"But they were evidence."

"Yes, they were. And since they actually contained the stuff that had started Catesby off on his whole spree, I just decided it would be better if they weren't available."

"Did Catesby know you'd got rid of them?"

He paused. "I think maybe I told him. Yes, I did."

"You missed one," Verity said. "We found it."

Barnwell shrugged. "Did you now? Well, we all make mistakes."

There was a pause.

"Do we have any other questions?" Cecilia said.

"Yes," Sir Marcus said, "we do."

She watched the small screen as the magistrate leaned forward in his chair.

"Ex-Detective Superintendent Barnwell," he said, "you are by your own testimony a liar, an accessory to murder, and one who has impeded the course of justice for personal gain. What convincing reason can you give me to believe that you are telling us the truth now?"

"I've already said — I'm a dying man. And much of my testimony is against myself. Why on earth should I lie to you?"

"For no obvious material reason, I grant you. And I grant that your DNA, when we have taken it and checked it against evidence from the crime scenes, may well indicate that you were involved in the deaths of both Frank Kermode and James Farthing, and therefore know a great deal about the events surrounding those deaths. Nevertheless, I am going to suggest a rather different narrative from the one you have given us. I put it to you that you yourself killed both these young men, that Gregory Catesby's touching the rope that hanged young Farthing was mere bad luck — perhaps happening much as, I gather, his solicitor suggested it could have happened when Catesby was being interviewed by the police — and that at this late stage, hearing of this, you have now *invented* this story of his involvement in the murders. And why? Because you loathe Gregory Catesby and everything he stands for: something you have in effect been telling us throughout your entire testimony—'the arsehole Catesby' you call him, with his 'la-di-da accent' from his 'posh school.' What better triumph could you have, dying yourself, than to strike down, virtually from beyond the grave, this symbol of all that you despise? And that, I suggest, is why you are now lying to us about this man who has, so far as everything else we know about him tells us, been throughout his life a model citizen, a generous benefactor of the poor, and a good friend to all, high and low."

Cecilia exchanged a glance with Verity, who raised her eyebrows and grimaced. A stretch, perhaps, but as a spur-of-the-moment reconstruction it wasn't at all bad, and given counsel for the defense approached a jury in the right way, they might well find it credible.

But Barnwell had, it seemed, an answer of his own.

He struggled to raise himself a little in the bed—the nurse stepped forward and adjusted the bed and the pillows for him—and then he stared directly at the tiny screen.

"Obviously," he said, and his voice was actually somewhat firmer, "you listened to some of what I told you, but not to all. Listen again while I spell this out. In 1994, following the deaths of Frank Kermode and James Farthing, Major Henry Catesby paid into a Swiss bank account in my name first half a million pounds and then, a day or so later, two million pounds. The account numbers and details are all at my bank in Málaga, and I give you full authority to look at them. If the police will also check Major Catesby's own records, which they surely can, I'm quite sure they'll find details of those transactions from his side. Now, unless you think the Major paid me two and a half million pounds in 1994 as part of a plot so that twenty-one years later I could tarnish the name of his son, you must surely see that what I'm telling you at this moment is the truth. He paid me that money to shut me up."

He sank back onto the pillow.

Cecilia looked back at the screen. Sir Marcus had been listening with eyes closed and his fingers together. After a moment his eyes opened. Slowly, he nodded.

"Yes," he said finally, "if the records are as you say they are, I think that *might* just convince me that on this occasion you are telling the truth, and perhaps it might convince a jury, too. It's hard to say." He paused. "Your confession, Barnwell, reminds me of Edmund's confession in *King Lear* – too late to be of use to any of the people whose lives you've ruined, but it may be of service to your own soul. I pray that it is. I have no further questions."

There was another pause. Cecilia looked their colleagues on screen, and then at Verity. "Is there anything else?"

"We do need that DNA sample," Verity said.

"There's plenty in there for the taking," Barnwell said, pointing to the basket full of used tissues beside his bed, "but for form's sake" – he pulled a clean tissue out of a packet on the bedside table and spat into it – "here you are. You've seen me give it."

Verity pulled on plastic gloves, took the tissue from him, and placed it in an evidence bag, which she labeled and put into her shoulder bag.

"Of course you already know it's going to be a match for the blood spatter on the boy's clothes?" he said.

"Of course we do," Verity said. "But we like to have everything tidy."

"Are there other questions?" Cecilia said.

The three in England looked at each other, there were headshakes, and they looked back at the camera.

"I think that we're done here," Glyn Davies said. "Do you have more, Detective Superintendent?"

Cecilia looked at Verity, who shook her head.

"We're done too, sir," she said.

She glanced at the clock.

"Interview concluded at 11:37 a.m.," she added for the

benefit of the recording, and then, turning to Agente González, "Gracias, Agente. Esto ha sido de mucha ayuda, pero creo que ya hemos terminado."

Agente González nodded politely. "Sí, detective superinten-dente." He switched off his equipment, and began gathering it together.

Barnwell watched him for a moment, and then turned to Cecilia. "Will you answer a question for me?" he said.

"That depends on what it is."

"What led you to reopen the case after all this time?"

"Technically it was never closed. But you know that." She paused, and gave a little smile. "I suppose you could say it's because my husband fell in love with a cockney sparrow who never stopped believing in her son."

"You mean Farthing's mother? Jenny Farthing?"

"You remember her?"

"Of course I do. I liked her. And she was still a bit of a looker even in her forties. I'm sorry she and her old man got so hurt by all this. And of course I was sorry about what happened to their boy. I never intended any of that."

Verity blew out her cheeks but said nothing.

"So your old man is a copper, too, is he?" Barnwell said to Cecilia.

"Hardly. He's an Anglican priest."

"A *priest*? Jesus Christ!"

"Anyway," she said, "you seem to have a beautiful life for yourself as a result of it all. As I said, we've seen your house!"

"Have you?" he said. "Well, the villa is beautiful, I'll give you that. But as for my life—I thought with two and a half million pounds in the bank it *would* be beautiful, but it's hardly turned out that way. My wife's left me. So have both my sons. So has my daughter. I haven't seen any of them for years and they won't come near me. And I'm dying. That's my beautiful life."

***

"I could almost feel sorry for him." Cecilia said when they were outside again in the sunshine

"So could I," Verity said, "though why on earth he'd expect his life to be beautiful when he knew it was rotten to the core is a mystery to me."

Forty-Eight

The offices of the Crown Prosecution Service, Longbrook House, New North Road, Exeter. The same afternoon.

"So my question is, do we now have enough? Should I have Gregory Catesby arrested and charged with murder?"

Chief Superintendent Glyn Davies was in the Exeter offices of the Crown Prosecution Service. Facing him were David Llewellyn, QC, who was based here in Exeter, and, on the wall screen opposite him via satellite, Charlene Hethcott, QC, from the CPS's southwest headquarters in Bristol.

As those who regularly watched a popular television series on crime fighting in London could probably have said in their sleep, in the British criminal justice system the people were represented by two separate yet equally important groups, "the police who investigate crime, and the Crown prosecutors who prosecute the offenders." Convenient and memorable though this summary was, it had, as Glyn had pointed out to Olwen while they were watching an old episode a few nights ago, two weaknesses, one of them perhaps more serious than the other.

The less serious was that it glossed over quite significant differences between England and Wales on the one hand and Scotland on the other. The more serious was that it did not make clear—indeed, some early episodes in the series seemed to him actually to imply the opposite—that in England and Wales it was finally the responsibility of the police, not the lawyers, to decide in any particular case whether or not someone should be charged and prosecuted.

Which meant, in the matter of Gregory Catesby, that the decision was his.

Certainly that didn't mean that in coming to that decision he wouldn't ask the advice of his legal colleagues. Indeed, as he had also said to Olwen, "it would be damned silly not to—not least because if it goes to court they are the poor blighters who are going to have to argue it!"

To that end, this morning, as soon as the interview with Barnwell was over, he'd uploaded the file with it to the Exeter CPS office and to CPS southwestern headquarters in Bristol, together with files on the whole case, and arranged to confer with them that afternoon.

For his part, he'd been fairly sure even after watching Cecilia's initial interview with Catesby that the man was guilty, even though the evidence against him was insufficient to bring into court. And now, following Cecilia and Verity's interview with ex-DSI Barnwell, he felt quite certain about it. But did CPS think they had enough to get a conviction?

David Llewellyn was inclined to caution.

"The fact is," he said, "apart from Barnwell's testimony, everything else you have is circumstantial. And the trouble with a dead man's dying testimony, even though it's admissible, is that no one can cross-examine it. Which is actually a gift for the other side, if they use it properly."

Charlene Hethcott from Bristol took a different line.

"You're right," she said to David, "but Barnwell *might* still live long enough so that if it came to trial it would be possible for him to testify live by satellite—as DSI Cavaliere suggested he might this morning. He seemed willing enough. And that might be an argument for getting on with it—for arresting Catesby and charging him now, and going for an early trial date. That way defense could cross-examine Barnwell—and of course prosecution could reexamine."

They looked at each other.

"Even so it's a risk," David from Exeter said.

Charlene from Bristol chuckled.

"Of course it's a risk!" she said. "Every trial's a risk. That's why we call it 'a trial,' isn't it? Unless perhaps you'd prefer the North Korean system?"

"I'm not denying any of that," the local man said, "but you still have to assess the degree of risk! I'm merely pointing out that while there *is* a *prima facie* case against your man, I'm not at all sure that a good defense counsel couldn't sow enough doubt in the minds of a jury to stop them convicting. Marcus Snowball's question showed that. *Reasonable doubt*, and all that."

He paused.

"That said," he added, looking to his colleague in Bristol on the screen, "I do take your point about going for an early trial if you *do* decide to charge him. It would be better from everyone's point of view—better for justice, frankly—if Barnwell's testimony were live."

"Ah, yes," Charlene from Bristol said, "justice! In the thrill of courtroom combat, one tends to forget that little element is supposed to be part of the system."

"I rather thought," Glyn said, "it was supposed to be the point of it?"

She smiled. "Yet the court is in some ways set up as a combat. The theory being that in a fight between truth and falsehood, the truth will win."

"Which works fairly well on the whole," David added, "unless of course both sides are lying—as happens quite often in civil suits." He paused. "It's particularly true of traffic. I remember when I was a young barrister going home after a day in court thinking, 'I've spent the entire day listening to sad stories of motorists who were always sober, always vigilant, never exceeded the speed limit, never broke any traffic law, and on the particular occasion that concerned the court were actually driving especially carefully in vehicles that were in perfect mechanical condition. And yet somehow or other they all managed to run into something!"

"Or into each other!" Charlene interjected.

"Or into each other! Now wasn't that amazing?'"

Charlene laughed. "So let's thank God," she said, "for the refreshing clarity of criminal justice, where we say to the defendants, 'You done it!' and they say, 'We never did!' and generally speaking either they're right or we are."

There was a pause.

Glyn gazed quizzically at his two colleagues. "So," he said slowly, "if I'm hearing you correctly, your joint response to the question, 'Should I have Gregory Catesby arrested and charged with murder?' is a definite 'perhaps'?"

If either was embarrassed, neither showed it.

"That's right," David said.

Charlene nodded.

"But," Glyn continued, "I'm also hearing you say, if I *am* going to do it, then I'd be well-advised to get on with it?"

They both nodded.

What thou doest, do quickly!

It was not, he reflected, the happiest precedent he could have imagined.

He sighed. "All right. I'm going to take all this as a cautious 'yes.' I'll have Catesby taken into custody and charged. Let's see what happens."

FORTY-NINE

Heavitree Police Station, Exeter. Thursday 12ᵗʰ November, 2015.

By the time Cecilia and Verity arrived back in Exeter on Thursday events had moved on: the main event that interested them being that, following the chief superintendent's conference with the Crown prosecutors, Gregory Eric Catesby had been arrested and charged with two murders.

"Frankly," Cecilia said, "Catesby still baffles me. After all that Joseph has dug up about his life, and then taking into consideration what Barnwell testified about him and our own evidence, it's as if we were dealing with two entirely different people."

Glyn Davies shrugged.

"What will happen to him?" Verity said. "When he committed those crimes he was technically a minor, wasn't he?"

"I suppose so, technically," Davies said. "But they may decide to try him as an adult anyway. He was only *just* a minor."

"I'm still not sure that there's enough," Verity said.

Again the chief superintendent shrugged. "Neither, to be frank, am I. Neither is CPS. But it's probably the best we can do. Anyway, everyone's very pleased with what you two pulled off in Spain. Full marks!"

The two women looked at each other.

"I'm not sure we did anything much," Verity said.

"Our *main* achievement," Cecilia said, "was to be chatted up by some very handsome Spanish policemen—"

"Not to mention an ageing but still gallant judge with a definite twinkle in his eye," Verity inserted.

"Exactly!" Cecilia said. "Well, the judge was your conquest, really. I just stood there looking submissive and demure—"

Joseph guffawed, a reaction that Cecilia chose to ignore.

"—and naturally," she continued, "we seized the opportunity to eat some very good food. Sea bream tartare with cider vinegar was something we both had a bit of a crush on, wasn't it?"

"Yum," Verity said.

"Exactly. Indeed, one might go so far as to say *profound* yum."

"Indeed one might," Verity said.

"So you see we haven't done anything much at all."

"Well, no," Davies said, "I can see that." (There was perhaps no need, Cecilia reflected, for him to agree *quite* so quickly.) "But these international link-ups can go wrong. This one went without a hitch. And at least to some extent, that has to be down to you two. So—full marks anyway!"

FIFTY

The Dog and Duck Inn, Exeter. Friday 13th November, 2013.

Last-minute babysitting arrangements were made and the team—ten people in all, for Olwen and Michael had been invited and Headley and Tom brought girlfriends Sue and Brenda—met for a Serious-Crimes-Team drink at eight o'clock the following evening at the Dog and Duck, a large, pleasant pub in Pemberton Street behind the Heavitree Station, which over recent months had become something of a local for the police.

The group was cheerful over beer and good pub food at a large table in one corner until about nine o'clock, at which point they became gradually aware that the main bar, which had been heaving in its normal cheery way with a Friday night crowd, had fallen strangely silent. After a while Glyn Davies got up and went to see what was happening. He stood for several minutes, watching, then came back to them, his face grave.

"I'm sorry to spoil the evening," he said, "but I'm afraid there's some very disturbing news on television. That's why it's gone quiet."

The others followed him back to the bar. There was a large television screen on the wall at the end, and gradually they registered what was coming through. The news was from Paris.

Clearly, some form of organized terrorist attack was in progress. People had been killed in restaurants and a concert hall. Suicide bombers had blown themselves up. The BBC reporter said the French emergency services reckoned there had to be at least a hundred dead, many of them young—ordinary folk at the beginning of a weekend, out for a meal or a drink with friends, or listening to music.

"Oh, dear God, those poor people," Verity said.

Cecilia found herself holding Michael's hand very tightly.

They watched for some moments longer in silence, and then as by mutual consent returned to their table.

"Jesus Christ," Headley said, abruptly breaking the silence, "when the hell will we have had enough of killing?"

"We?" Tom said.

"Us! The human race! We solve a couple of murders and then some maniacs who claim they've got God on their side go and commit a hundred more. It makes me feel like giving up."

Tom nodded. "I know how you feel."

"I'm sure you do," Glyn Davies said quietly, "and I doubt there'll be an end to murders or murdering any time soon. But I'd say that's precisely the reason why you *shouldn't* give up. You're good coppers, both of you. And don't be in any doubt about it: you *do* help keep some measure of peace. Of course it's not perfect. But it's still a damned sight better than chaos. And it is, incidentally, a damned sight better here than most other places I can think of. Which is why everyone wants to live here."

"Well I'm not giving up," Verity said, raising her glass. "Ce soir je suis parisienne! Vive la France!"

True to form, her accent was atrocious.

Cecilia reached out and took her free hand. "Amen to that, sweet friend," she said. "Me, too. Vive la France!"

As the news from Paris was breaking, Gregory Catesby was in the process of being transferred from the police station in Heavitree, where he had originally been arrested and remanded in custody, to the main Exeter prison in New North Road.

Three officers were charged with his transfer, which should, and in normal circumstances no doubt would, have been straightforward enough. Perhaps there was some confusion in the instructions they had been given. More likely they were distracted by the news from France, for it was after they had placed Catesby in a police van that, summoned by colleagues, they left him alone, each assuming that the others had seen to it that he and the van were properly secured, none of them in his distraction thinking to check that assumption.

It was only when they saw each other gathered round the television screen that they realized what they had done, or rather omitted to do, and returned in haste.

Too late.

They'd left him unsupervised for only a few minutes, but it had been enough.

They arrived to find the van empty and their charge gone.

FIFTY-ONE

Saturday, 14th November.

The Exeter police were at first spared some embarrassment over losing a man in custody because the following day all eyes of the media were on Paris. Which was in fact no consolation at all. The day remained a day of utter frustration, only compounded by the grief of their French colleagues.

Of course steps were taken to recover the fugitive.

All Catesby's known haunts were checked: the golf club first, as was to be expected, but also Saint Loye's House, the Save the Children shop, and even the Blue Sovereign recovery home, though if Joseph's information was correct—and knowing Joseph, it probably was—Catesby did not even know where it was. His photograph was circulated and his description broadcast. There were roadblocks on every road out of Exeter, even the minor ones. A National Police Air Service Eurocopter made repeated sweeps of the city and the surrounding area.

All with no result.

Somehow, it seemed, Gregory Catesby had managed to vanish from everyone's sight.

At about nine o'clock in the evening, at the end of a long and apparently wasted day, Cecilia was sent home to get some rest, and other officers took over from her.

She and Michael ate a late supper together and then checked on the children. The last thing to be done was to take Figaro for his final walk. They were preparing to do this together when the telephone rang.

Cecilia pointed at Figaro. "I'll take Fig out. You deal with that and then we can go to bed."

Michael nodded vigorously as he picked up the phone.

Outside it was a pleasant evening, and mild for the time of year. A slight wind moved the trees.

Cecilia and Figaro walked slowly to the gate, and unlatched it. She stifled a yawn. Dear God, she was tired.

Part of her registered that there was a car parked across the street—a Peugeot, dark-colored, with the driver's-side window down. But her main attention was directed toward Figaro, who, ears and tail firmly fixed in his "I-am-concentrating" position, was carrying out a careful inspection of messages left during the day on the lamppost to the right of the rectory gate. After this he would no doubt be leaving his own personal statement for the evening.

From his point of view, she thought as she stood waiting for this ritual to be completed, I suppose it's like me checking my email or seeing what there is for me on Facebook.

But then, suddenly and unexpectedly, Figaro looked up and across the street. His hackles rose, he uttered an angry growl, and moved between Cecilia and the road.

"Bitch!" came from the car in a voice she seemed to recognize.

A flash.

A bang.

And something hit her in the chest.

FIFTY-TWO

St Mary's Rectory. Seconds later.

Michael had answered his caller's question and was replacing the handset when he heard the bang, and then Figaro barking furiously.

He rushed out to find Cecilia on her back, bleeding from her chest, and Figaro going mad beside her.

He had just enough presence of mind to drag out his mobile phone and, with trembling fingers, to call 999.

"Ambulance. St Mary's Rectory, Church Road," he said. "I think my wife's been shot."

What did he mean, "think"? He knew bloody well she'd been shot.

"I'll get someone there, sir," the dispatcher said.

He fell to his knees beside Cecilia, with Figaro close to him, whimpering. He could tell she was struggling to breathe, and sensed she was trying to speak. He had never felt so utterly helpless in his life or so utterly terrified. He could only kneel there, holding her hand and stroking her hair and muttering platitudes. "We're here, darling. Help's on the way. I love you. It's going to be all right."

Just how long it took he never knew, but it was probably only minutes before he heard sirens whose cry was to him at that moment a benediction.

Now there were flashing lights and an ambulance.

A police car.

Medics and police officers.

"Christ, it's DSI Cavaliere and Father Michael," one of the officers said. "Let the station know, Brenda!"

"On it," she said and began talking into her mobile.

"I was inside on the phone," Michael said. "Cecilia had gone to walk Fig. I just heard a bang and came out."

One of the medics was now kneeling opposite him. "What's her name?"

Michael looked up at him blankly. For a moment, he seemed to have lost the power of speech. Then—

"Oh! Cecilia. She's Cecilia!"

"Cecilia!" the medic called. "Can you hear me, Cecilia? Stay with me, Cecilia!"

"I think, sir," the other medic said to Michael, getting him gently to his feet, "it'll be best if we can get the dog into the house. Otherwise he'll try to follow the ambulance."

"Our children are in there, too," Michael said. "They're asleep—I hope."

"I'll get the dog inside," the PC called Brenda said, switching off her mobile. She'd already picked up Figaro's lead and it was immediately obvious she was one of those people who have a way with dogs. Michael had a vague sense that he knew her. Wasn't she Tom Wilkin's girlfriend from the pub last night?

"I can stay there and keep an eye on the children for the moment if you like," she said. "Is there someone I can call for you?"

"Cecilia's parents," he said. "Their number's programmed into the hall phone."

"I'll deal with it," she said. "Go with your wife."

He turned back to Cecilia.

The medics were now kneeling on each side of her. The one who'd asked her name was talking fast into a mobile. "She's been shot. Severe chest wound. Internal hemorrhaging. She's got a pulse but it's threading."

The other put a breathing mask over Cecilia's face. Seconds later she was on a stretcher and they were loading her into the ambulance. The other continued giving instructions to the hospital. "We've done everything we can here. We're leaving now. We should be with you in ten minutes max."

Michael got in beside her.

Cecilia lay still and white.

He was numb.

FIFTY-THREE

Joseph and Verity's house.

Verity's mobile was vibrating under her pillow. She sat up and pulled it out, doing her best not to wake Joseph.

"DI Jones," she said softly.

It was the chief superintendent. "Verity, we have a crisis and I need everyone. Someone just shot Cecilia outside their house. It must be Catesby."

"Oh my God! Is she—" She stopped.

"I don't know," he said. "She's on her way to the hospital. Michael's with her. That's all I know. But we have to catch this bloody lunatic."

"I'm on my way sir."

Joseph was by now awake. Verity told him the news quickly and quietly as she moved about the bedroom pulling on clothes.

Samuel, when she glanced into his cot, was blissfully asleep.

But Hoover, on her little bed by the wardrobe, was starting to wriggle into life.

"Samuel's still zonked," she said, "but I think Hoover's about to have a wobble attack."

Joseph got up and gathered the wriggling mass of affection into his arms.

Verity collected her warrant card and her keys, zipped her

jacket, and kissed him. But then for a moment she clung to him, squashing Hoover between them.

"Oh God, this is awful," she said.

"I know."

Hoover wriggled up between them and licked her chin. She smiled in spite of herself, but there were tears in her eyes.

"I know it's awful," Joseph said. "But now you must be strong — for Cecilia."

She nodded, and let him go.

"I know," she said quietly. "I will."

FIFTY-FOUR

The Royal Devon and Exeter Hospital, Wonford Road.
About the same time.

They let Michael stay with Cecilia until they were in the hospital and wheeling her towards the theatre.

"You'll have to leave us now, Father," the nurse said. "We'll let you know as soon as we have news."

"She wouldn't want me to leave her," he said, conscious that he was babbling.

"No," the man in white who was walking beside her said gently, "she probably wouldn't. But I'm the one who's got to remove the bullet that's about two centimeters from her heart, so just at the moment it's what *I* want that matters. And I really do want you to leave, so I can concentrate on doing my job."

"Of course you do. I'm sorry. I'll get out of your way."

"No apology necessary. Just trust us to do everything we can."

They wheeled Cecilia away.

A little nurse was standing beside him. "Now you come and sit down in our waiting room over here," she said, "and I'll bring you a nice cup of tea. Believe me, Father, our Mr. Goldstein is the best there is. Your good lady couldn't be in better hands."

"Thank you," he said. "I'm sure she couldn't."

He entered the waiting room, which was empty, and sat down. He closed his eyes and did his best to direct his thoughts.

Dear God, be with her, help her as she needs, not as I think of her but as you know her to be.

After a while he opened his eyes again and looked around him.

It was unusual for the waiting room to be empty. Generally there were several people waiting. He'd been in here before—surely more often than most people—but always as pastor, always supporting others who were worried or frightened. At least, he hoped he was being supportive.

Here was the nurse with the tea.

"There you are, Father, nice and hot. Now you just enjoy it and try not to worry."

"Thank you, nurse."

It was milky and very sweet, not at all how he usually drank it. But just now, for some reason, the sweetness was comforting. He sipped it gratefully.

On the wall opposite him was a large Great Western Railway poster.

Penzance.

One Saturday during the summer, he and Cecilia had planned to take Rachel on the train down from Exeter to Penzance. The most beautiful railway journey in the world—that was what everyone said it was. But then at the last minute there had been the funeral of a devoted parishioner that he had to take, and so Cecilia and Rachel had to go alone.

"I'll go with you next time," he'd said.

FIFTY-FIVE

Heavitree Police Station. Twenty minutes later.

"So far as I can tell," Glyn Davies said to Verity when she arrived at the Heavitree station, "during the day, Catesby must have walked cross-country the two or three miles from Exeter to the golf club and then laid low until it was dark. That's why our searches and roadblocks didn't get him. We also had officers watching his flat at the golf club. But then, lo and behold, there's a sudden fire in a greenhouse near the course, and so everyone, including our gallant officers who are supposed to be watching the flat, rushes out to see what is happening and help put it out. Obviously, Catesby started it."

Verity raised her eyebrows.

"I know," he said. "The oldest trick in the book and it worked like a charm. Anyway, while they were all outside playing at being the fire brigade, Catesby breaks into his flat and then goes down to the yard and takes his car. When our people got back they found the door to the flat open and the desk drawers pulled open too."

"Damn. And presumably that's where he had a gun stashed?"

"Presumably. The good news is, at least we now know what we're looking for. His car's a dark red Peugeot RCT GT, and we have the registration."

The phone on his desk buzzed. He picked up the handset and listened. "Right. Then that's the area to search in." He replaced the handset and looked at her. "An ANPR camera picked it up a up a few minutes ago. He was turning off Alphington Road onto Church Road, going south."

Verity hesitated only a moment. "Shillingford Abbot! St. Loye's House! That's where he's headed. It's one of his haunts. I was there this afternoon."

"Are you up to going back there now?"

"Yes, sir. I am."

"There's an armed response unit ready to go with you. We know he's dangerous, and presumably still armed, so I'm not taking any chances, and I don't want you to."

"Right, sir."

FIFTY-SIX

On the road to Shillingford Abbot. Some minutes later.

The two police Mercedes-Benz Sprinter vans with their compliment of armed officers drove swiftly the few miles toward Shillingford Abbot and St. Loye's, emergency lights flashing and what little other traffic there was on the road scattering before them. Then, when they were minutes away from their target, Verity, seated next to the driver of the first van, ordered them turn off all their emergency lights.

"When we arrive," she said, "we deploy as quietly as possible."

It was a possible hostage situation, but she didn't want to create the very standoff they were trying to avoid.

The sergeant—a stocky, grizzled man whose name, according to his nametag, was Coulter and who was, she suspected, ex-army—nodded.

"Understood, ma'am."

The two vans arrived at the big double gates of Saint Loye's House a few minutes later, and the armed officers deployed in commendable silence.

She immediately noticed a dark Peugeot RCZ GT that had been parked near a streetlight just past the gates. In the sodium-yellow glare she wasn't entirely sure of the color, but then the beam of her flashlight picked up the license plate. She looked at Sergeant Coulter, who nodded. It checked. The car was Catesby's.

She shone her flashlight into it, but there was nothing to be seen but empty seats and a newspaper.

"Let's check the boot," she said.

It was empty.

"Should a couple of us keep an eye on it, ma'am, in case he somehow tries to get back to it and pull a fast one?"

Verity nodded. "Good thought, Sergeant. Make it so. The rest with me."

Sergeant Coulter detailed two of his people to watch Catesby's car and their own vehicles.

Verity walked back to the big double gates and pressed the buzzer, the armed response officers standing around her. After a minute there was a click. From the speaker there came a fragile, somewhat tired voice.

"St. Loye's House. I am Father Aidan. Who is this?"

"This is Detective Inspector Jones, Exeter CID."

"Really, Inspector, it's the middle of the night!"

"Father," she said, "this isn't a courtesy call. Open up."

FIFTY-SEVEN

Outside St Mary's Rectory.

It had felt at first as if she'd been punched in the chest.
Cecilia fell back against the garden wall and thence to the pavement. There she lay gasping, unable to move. The pain in her chest grew worse, like a huge weight pressing down on her.

She was aware of Figaro standing over her, barking defiantly.

Dear Figaro.

Now Michael was by her.

She sensed his panic and his love and tried to speak. But she couldn't. She was finding it harder and harder to breathe.

He was on his phone. She wished she could move to reassure him.

Now there were sirens and lights and urgent voices.

A man's voice was calling her, "Cecilia! Cecilia!"

But it seemed to be getting farther off.

Gradually, it melted away . . .

And like this insubstantial pageant faded . . .

Into soft light, and silence.

The silence deepened and the light became brighter, a shining tunnel drawing her to itself.

Slowly, slowly.

Ever more intense.

Deeper.

Until in an instant she was through it and on the other side, standing on a hillside in brilliant sunshine.

The pain in her chest had gone. Indeed, she felt fit and strong.

The air around her was warm, the warmth of the Italian *mezzogiorno*. Yet there were birds singing and somehow it felt like England, too. To her left, far beneath where she stood, she could see the sea, calm and sparkling, stretching to a blue horizon. She felt at peace, as if she were in the holiest of shrines, and yet excited, as if she were setting out on the most thrilling of adventures. She sighed with delight.

There was a sudden mild commotion behind her. She turned.

Bounding toward her through long grass came an enormous dog, large, cream-colored, and enthusiastic, tail waving like an aerial through the fronds.

"Lazarus!" she cried and seconds later was rolling with him on the ground in a joyous, playful bundle, hugging his animal strength and being licked and gently buffeted in return.

"I see, child," came a man's voice with a slight German accent from above her and somewhat to her right, "that your old friend has found you even before I did!"

She sat up, with the mighty Lazarus leaning against her, warm and solid, panting.

"Lazarus was my friend when I was a little girl," she said.

"I know."

The man wore a black cloak and was of medium height, with dark hair and a dark beard touched with gray. He seemed a little past his youth.

And she would have known him anywhere.

"Oh, Father Spee!" she said. "How lovely to see you!"

FIFTY-EIGHT

Saint Loye's House. A few minutes later.

While Verity and the armed response team waited, there was a turning of keys and a rattling of bolts, and then the double gates opened. There in the entrance stood Father Aidan, small and frail.

Verity did not waste words. "You have a fugitive. Where is he, Father?"

"In the chapel, Detective."

"Is he armed? Was he carrying a gun?"

"Not that I saw."

"How many exits are there from the chapel?"

"Just the two that you see—the main one and the side door."

Verity nodded to Sergeant Coulter, who detailed officers to cover both.

"No one goes in or out," she said. "Deadly force is the absolute last resort, but Catesby's already shot one person tonight, and you must use deadly force to restrain him if you have to."

"Understood, ma'am."

"Now, Sergeant Coulter," she said quietly, "who is your steadiest man?"

"Jardine, ma'am," he said without hesitation.

"Which is he?"

He turned. "Constable Jardine!"

"Yes, Sergeant." A young man stepped forward.

Verity nodded. "Thank you, Sergeant. Constable Jardine, you are with me. We'll go in, just the two of us. Sergeant, I'll leave my mobile open, so you can hear what happens. Come if I call you. If you hear things starting to go bad use your discretion."

"Understood, ma'am."

"Father Aidan, stay here with the officers." She paused, only for a second. "Let's do it, Constable Jardine. As soon as we're inside and identify the suspect, cover him with your weapon."

"Yes, ma'am."

FIFTY-NINE

"Cecilia Anna Maria!" Father Spee said. "It is lovely for me to see you, too. You are more beautiful than ever. But come, I have something to show you."

Her companion and mentor from other adventures bent down and, grasping her hand, swept her lightly to her feet.

"This way," he said. "It isn't far."

They walked through long grass and buttercups in the sunshine, with Lazarus bounding along beside them. And just to walk thus was a delight. After a while they came to trees, ash, elm and oak, tall and graceful, with soft banks of grass between them.

And now everywhere she looked there were people sleeping on the grass, breathing softly. Occasionally, one of them would move a little, but always they looked peaceful. Their dreams, if they had them, were wholesome and refreshing.

"Who are these?" she asked.

"Who do you think they are? Look at them."

She peered at a young man lying near her. Wait! She had seen that face somewhere—in a photograph, surely—

"It's James Farthing," she said.

He nodded.

There was a boy beside him.

"Frank Kermode!" she said.

"They died before their time. But death—even untimely

death—does not have the last word. They rest in peace and they will rise in glory."

"So the grief is all forgotten?"

"Not forgotten—never that! Even our Beloved still bears his scars. But it is transfigured."

"And what about James Farthing's friend—Julie? I don't see her."

He smiled. "Before she died, Julie was already very far advanced in our Beloved's service, farther than anyone except our Beloved knew. Farther than she knew herself! So in death she needed no renewing and cleansing sleep but already progresses from glory to glory."

"Were you like that?" Cecilia said.

He looked at her and laughed. "Oh, Cecilia Anna Maria! What a question! I only know that I am here, my sins forgiven, by grace of the Beloved. No one can say more—or less!"

And now as they walked farther into the forest it seemed to Cecilia that by some gift of sight she could see deeper and farther, and was ever more aware of the infinite number of those who slept and were renewed—men and women of every race, creed, and clime.

At one point there was a group, a hundred or so, who lay together. "Paris?" she said, hardly knowing why.

He nodded. "Here sleep most of those who died. A few, like Julie, were summoned at once to glory."

"And those who killed them? Are they here, too?"

"Those, too. They died committing a great evil, but they thought they were doing God's will."

She nodded.

"They have much to learn," he said, "as indeed have most of us. They were badly broken. But then—you remember the story of the repair shop?"

For a moment she was puzzled, but then she remembered! It was a story Michael told her when they were first going out together: about a time when he was working in Stepney, in the East End of London. There'd been a little Jewish repair shop in a side street near St. Dunstan's Church. A beaten-up old wreck of a place it was, with peeling paint and a window full of junk. He'd walked past it quite often on his way to the church. What he specially noticed about it though was not the mess in the window but a noticeboard that sat in the middle of the mess. A big square of white cardboard, and on it someone had printed with a thick blue crayon in large capital letters: "NOTHING IS BROKEN BEYOND REPAIR."

Sometimes, he told her, he'd stop in front of the shop and look at that notice and wonder.

Did they really believe that?

Nothing broken beyond repair?

Nothing?

She nodded.

"So they can be mended?" she said to Spee.

"They can. Our dear Gustav was right:

'*O glaube, mein Herz, o glaube:*

'*Es geht dir nichts verloren!*

'*O believe, my heart, O believe:*

'*Nothing is lost to you!*'"

And now her vision widened still further, and she saw not just men and women but beasts and birds and insects and plants and every living thing, lives more numerous than the stars — the whole unlikely miracle of carbon-based life, dependent for its very existence on the precise nature of the galaxy around it, so that even the tiniest blade of grass might in some sense claim, "For my sake, the worlds were made." That morning in the garden there'd been a little moth that somehow — God knew how — was caught in a bird feeder. She'd tried to free it. But its wings were torn and in the end she could only watch in useless sorrow as the tiny creature struggled to fly and fell, fluttering and helpless, doomed. But now for a second she felt sure she saw it again, its wings whole and strong, in its own degree magnificent, joyful, flying free.

"Every single life is precious," her guide said, answering her thought, "because in the beginning our Beloved saw all that had been made, *et erant valde bona*—and they were very good: all of them created in love, for love, and by love. And our Beloved has promised, *Et ego, si exaltatus fuero a terra*—and I, if I be lifted up from the earth—*omnia traham ad meipsum*—will draw all things to myself.'"

"So nothing will be lost?"

"Nothing will be lost that does not choose to be lost. None go to the dolorous city but those who wish to. Watch."

SIXTY

The chapel of St. Loye's House. A few minutes later.

Inside the chapel was decent Victorian gothic, with a soft but adequate religious light. And now Verity saw Gregory Catesby. He was on his knees at the side of the nave to her left, speaking into a confessional box.

She stopped where she was at the chapel entrance, careful to remain out of earshot of the confessional, and waited, signaling Jardine to do the same.

At length, Catesby crossed himself and stood up. A moment or so later the door to the confessional opened and a tall gray-haired monk came out.

He looked across at Verity and Constable Jardine, whose Heckler and Koch MP5 submachine gun now covered Catesby.

"I'm Detective Inspector Verity Jones, Exeter CID," she said, producing her warrant card. "And this is Constable Jardine."

The monk laid a hand on Catesby's shoulder. "And I am Father Austin, the warden of this house," he said. "This man has come to us seeking pastoral counsel and guidance."

"I understand that, Father," she said, "and I've tried to respect your sanctuary. Which is why I waited so that you could give Mr. Catesby absolution. But he has broken the law and he is a fugitive, so now he must come with us."

Father Austin nodded. "Detective Inspector, would it be satisfactory if I were to give you my word he'll surrender himself in the morning? Could he remain with us this one night? We intended to bring him to you in the morning anyway."

She shook her head. "I'm sure you did, Father, but the answer is 'no.' He's already escaped from custody once. And while he was at large he shot a colleague of mine, who may die."

The force of what she was saying came bitterly home to her, and for a moment she had to pause and swallow.

She bit her lip and resumed. "I dare say you may be able visit him tomorrow, although it isn't up to me to decide that. And he'll certainly have access to legal counsel. But for now I'm taking him into custody."

Father Austin seemed about to make another suggestion, but she held up her hand.

"This isn't a negotiation," she said quietly.

He nodded. "Of course not." He turned to Catesby. "You must go with the police officers, my son. You remain in our prayers, and, of course, we shall support you in every way we can."

Catesby nodded. "Thank you, Father. I'll do as you say."

He walked toward her. Plump and somewhat disheveled, he looked harmless enough, but she was in no mood to take chances.

"Stop where you are, Mr. Catesby," she said.

He stopped.

"Now, moving slowly, put your hands on your head and kneel down."

He did so.

"Now lie down on your front, face towards the floor."

As he complied, clumsily enough, she could hear in her head the voice of Cecilia. *Yes, I know it's awkward. Actually, it's meant to be.*

Jardine continued to cover him.

She spoke into her mobile. "I think we have the situation under control. Just two of you, come into the chapel now."

"Ma'am."

Seconds later the chapel door opened and the Sergeant Coulter and another constable entered. She nodded towards Catesby. "Cuff him, and check to see if he's carrying a weapon."

"Yes, ma'am," the sergeant said, and then, a few moments later, "He's clean."

"Good," she said. "Then get him up."

They brought Catesby to his feet.

"Well," she said to him, "at least you didn't bring a firearm into the chapel. So where is it?"

"It's in the car," he said, "the glove compartment. It's Daddy's old sidearm from the army."

She nodded.

"Put him in the van," she said, "and make sure he's secure this time, will you? Let's not have a repeat of Friday! And get the weapon from his car. Put it in evidence."

"Yes, ma'am."

The three officers went out with the re-arrested man.

There was a moment of silence.

Verity looked around her and took a deep breath. The chapel was a peaceful place despite all that had happened. It felt like a house of prayer. She liked it.

After a moment, Father Austin spoke.

"I'm deeply sorry about your colleague — the officer who was shot — I think perhaps a friend of yours?"

She turned and met his gaze. "Except for my husband, she is my closest friend. And in many ways my mentor."

"Oh dear. I am so sorry. She shall be in our prayers."

Verity nodded. "Thank you."

SIXTY-ONE

A nd now as Cecilia looked, the scope of her vision grew wider still, until even the countless dead were themselves only a precious but tiny part in the grandeur and beauty of the universe. She heard music, music she recognized, music that she and Michael had heard once before, the everlasting music, and she was happy.

"You have heard that before," he said.

She nodded. How, indeed, could she ever forget that she had heard it? But her heart was too full for her to speak.

Spee waited for a while and then said, "But now you must decide. Cecilia Anna Maria, will you go on, or will you go back?"

"Oh."

This was something she had not expected.

The truth was, at this moment she felt peace — peace in what Michael had once told her was the full meaning of the Hebrew word for peace: *shalom* — harmony, completeness. She knew what Lady Julian meant when she said, "All shall be well and all manner of thing shall be well" — and a part of that knowledge was her knowing it to be true not only for her but for Michael and Rachel and Rosina and every life in the universe, a destiny as richly and precisely designed, a glory as full and complete, as if that life were the only life there had ever been, and its perfection the sole purpose of creation. Except, of course, that it was *not* the only life there had ever been, but one of countless lives, and a part of its destined perfection was its calling to share in the everlasting dance, the limitless dialogue and fellowship of all lives, *communio sanctorum*, the communion of the holy.

The effect of this knowledge was not that she hesitated in her decision. She did not hesitate at all. But at the back of her mind she was aware, as one is aware of an interesting possibility, that she *might* have hesitated, and that to have done so would not have been wrong or unreasonable, even as she said, "This is beautiful, more beautiful than I could have imagined. But there are others that I love. I think they would like me to be there. I shall go back."

Spee nodded. "It is a good choice. Although while you are here, I am not sure that you can make a bad one."

"Though I do so hate to leave Lazarus again!" she added.

But Lazarus wagged his tail and Father Spee laughed. "Your old friend understands more than you imagine," he said. "Actually, he always did. Haven't you noticed that about the beasts? We understand things that are impossible for them, but they understand without effort things that we find hard, important things that take us a lifetime to grasp."

Lazarus wagged his tail again and Spee touched his head lightly.

"They too belong to our Beloved," he said. "They are not baptized, and they do not need to be, *quia et ipsa creatura liberabitur* — for the creature itself also shall be delivered — *a servitute corruptionis* — from the servitude of corruption — *in libertatem gloriae filiorum Dei* — into the liberty of the glory of the children of God. Lazarus will go to his place and sleep, and he will be here to greet you when you return."

Spee waited while Cecilia stroked Lazarus and was nuzzled in return. Then he stretched out his hand.

"Come, child," he said. "If you will go back, then it is time."

SIXTY-TWO

At the gates of St Loye's House. A few minutes later.

"You've made him secure?" Verity said to Sergeant Coulter when she got back to the van.

"Safe as houses, ma'am. He isn't going anywhere. Not unless he takes the side of the van and six of our lot down first, and I don't think he's quite up to that. And here" — he produced a plastic evidence bag with a handgun inside it — "is his weapon from the glove compartment: a 9mm Browning HP automatic. They were standard army issue until the eighties, so if his father was in the army it could well have been *Daddy's*, just like he said."

She peered at the weapon and nodded. "Good work, Sergeant."

"Thank you, ma'am. And if you don't mind me saying so — well done."

She looked at him in surprise.

"It was a tricky situation back there," he said. "You didn't know how he'd react or what was going to happen. Things could easily have gone pear-shaped. But you never lost your cool and we always knew exactly what we were supposed to be doing."

This was praise indeed from the professionals. Despite Verity's anxieties, she smiled. "Thank you, Sergeant."

He looked at her for a moment. Then he said, "Permission to speak freely, ma'am?"

"Yes, of course."

"I think, ma'am, that you don't like guns. And around armed response you're a little nervous because of that. Maybe even a little embarrassed?"

She hesitated. He was right, of course. "I suppose so — yes, I am."

"Well, you don't need to be! I don't *like* guns myself. I'm not too bad at using them, but that doesn't mean I like them. And I don't have much time for people who do. They generally have other faults."

"Oh." She hesitated. "I suppose what worries me is that when I tell your people, 'We may have to use deadly force,' I'm asking you to do something I'm not at all sure I'd be up to doing myself."

"You're not sure you could kill someone?"

"No, I'm not."

"Well, that's nothing to be ashamed of. You're a detective, not a soldier. So let's hope you never have to."

"Have you killed anyone, Sergeant?"

"When I was in the army, yes, ma'am, in Afghanistan. Never since, thank God, and I hope it stays that way. But you never know." He paused. "Every time you kill someone, two people die. The person you killed, and the person you were before you did it."

He looked hard at her.

"The fact remains, ma'am, you were good out there. I was confident in you, and so were my team."

Verity felt herself coloring at this praise. "Thank you, Sergeant Coulter. It's been my honor."

SIXTY-THREE

Sunday, 14th November, 2015.
The Royal Devon and Exeter Hospital, Wonford Road.
3:20 a.m.

Someone was shaking Michael gently by the shoulder.

He must have dozed off. He had a crick in his neck and his mouth was dry. But now Mr. Goldstein the surgeon was standing over him, looking tired but pleased.

"I believe your wife will be fine, Father. She's asleep now. We've removed the bullet. All is well."

Michael was so numb with tiredness and dread that for a moment he could scarcely register his own relief.

"Thank you," he said at last. "Thank you so very much. I don't know what to say."

The surgeon smiled. "You can come and see her if you like, though you mayn't speak to her."

"Oh, yes! Please! I would like."

As Michael got to his feet he saw that Cecilia's papa and Joseph were there in the room with him, sitting opposite. They, too, were smiling. How long had they been there, keeping him silent company? Faithful friends!

"I think," the surgeon said, looking at Papa, "that before we go you needed to tell Father Michael something?"

"Yes," Papa said. "It's just that we took the liberty of phoning the bishop about all this and he sends his love and prayers, and he says to tell you to be concerned about nothing except Cecilia, and he'll see to it that everything's taken care of in church today."

Oh Lord, it was Sunday.

Michael nodded and smiled weakly. "Thank you." He seemed to be saying that a lot lately.

Mr. Goldstein then walked with him through long corridors with bright white lights and white walls until at last they came to the ward in Intensive Care where Cecilia lay, surrounded by tubes and dials and monitors. There, he was able to sit by her bed and look at her.

It seemed to him that she had never looked more beautiful. Or was it that what had happened was causing him to look at her properly? As he had looked at her when he first knew her? When the sight of sunlight falling on her hair or the sound of her voice on the phone had made his heart beat faster? When they were in Sicily and she went swimming while he lay on the beach and he could hardly take his eyes off her? And then she'd come back and flopped down beside him on the sand and he'd tasted salt on her lips? Had he begun of late to take her for granted? To assume her presence in his life, as if it were something to which he had a right? Oh, dear God, let him not do that!

At any rate, for now he was happy just to sit and gaze at her, to watch her breathe and to thank God she did breathe.

Some time later, Mr. Goldstein came back.

"Go home now," he said, "and get some proper sleep. Come back later today. Let's say about four o'clock this afternoon. She should be awake by then, and she'll need you not to be exhausted."

"Thank you," Michael said. "I'll do that. You're a good man."

The surgeon smiled. "I try to be. Sometimes."

SIXTY-FOUR

The Royal Devon and Exeter Hospital. Some days later.

Cecilia's room was full of cards and kind thoughts. They'd come from friends and colleagues, from Michael's parishioners, from the bishop and the dean, from the mayor and the sheriff and the chief constable, from Sir Marcus Snowball and his sister Petronella, from the monks at St. Loye's and the residents of the Blue Sovereign. Others were from friends and acquaintances farther afield and of other times: Sergeant Wyatt and Mrs. Wyatt, Mother Evelyn and the sisters at St. Boniface Abbey, Mr. Pettigrew and his daughter Jennifer and the customers at the Great Western, Danny and Josie Kellog (who'd sent an *enormous* get-well card eighteen inches by twelve with a gold and purple border — trust Danny Kellog to be completely over the top!), the Reverend Doctor Susanna Metz in Petrockstowe and her rambunctious dog Lily, former colleagues in the Met and people all over the country and even some from abroad.

She would have a lot of thank-you letters to write.

There had also been features and articles about her on local television and in the West Country papers: some self-congratulatory in tone, pointing to the strictness of gun control laws in Britain and noting that without them, such as events as those of Saturday evening would surely be as commonplace here as they were in America; some lamenting what they perceived as a general increase in violent crime (as Joseph pointed out, in southwest England at least, the crime statistics did not actually support this perception); some merely praising police officers like Cecilia and the emergency services in general for the commitment they showed and the risks they took to preserve our lives and liberties.

No doubt it would all soon pass, but for these few days at least it seemed that DSI Cecilia Cavaliere was the West Country's heroine. For her part, recovering rapidly and almost back to her usual self — Mr. Goldstein had promised she could go home at the end of the week, although not back to work — she felt something between amusement and bemusement about the whole thing.

"All I actually *did* was take Figaro for a walk and get shot. How does that make me a heroine?" She looked at Michael and giggled and took his hand. "Surely you haven't forgotten Cyril Strathcott-Brown?" she said.

He stared at her for a moment and then started to chuckle, too — although they did then have to explain the joke to everyone else.

Cyril Strathcott-Brown was a former soldier from World War II whom Michael had come to know when he was curate in his first parish. In 1940, then Second Lieutenant Cyril Strathcott-Brown, nineteen years old, barely out of school and green as grass, he'd found himself assigned to the command of a night patrol, a dozen or so young men barely older or more experienced than himself, dangerously near to the German front lines. Fortunately for him and the rest of them, they were accompanied by a tough, experienced sergeant, a cockney, whose name was William Taylor and who actually knew what he was doing. Forty or so years on, Cyril Strathcott-Brown still treasured the words Sergeant Taylor said to him as they set out. "Now then, young sir, you keep your 'ead down! And that goes for all of you. Any bloody fool can get 'isself shot!"

"So what does that make me?" Cecilia said amid laughter, although to tell the truth her visitors that morning were such a noisy, cheerful group—Michael himself, together with Verity and Joseph and Glyn Davies—almost in party mood, that it took very little to make them laugh.

"So what's happening to Gregory Catesby?" she said when they had stopped laughing. "I hope you haven't gone and mislaid him again! To lose him *once*," she added, slipping into her best Dame Edith Evans takeoff, "may be regarded as a misfortune; to lose him twice would begin to look like *carelessness!*"

Michael laughed out loud.

But then as she watched them, the four looked uncertainly at each other.

Obviously, the hospital had told them she was not to be involved with matters connected to work that might stress her. But she really felt fine and she was madly curious.

"Oh, come on," she said, "if you don't tell me *anything* about what's going on, I think it's quite likely I shall get *really* stressed out. And then, of course," she added in a sudden fit of manipulative genius, "I'll tell my new friend Mr. Goldstein how you've all upset me and probably set my recovery back months, if not years, and then he'll be absolutely furious with all of you!"

Glyn Davies looked at her and then at the others, gave a half-smile and shrugged. "All right, since you insist, here are the basic facts. Gregory Catesby is safely in custody, undergoing psychiatric evaluation prior to a decision about judicial proceedings."

"In other words," Verity said, "is he bad or is he bonkers? My money is on bonkers."

"The good news," Davies added, "is that he's now admitted to everything—the two earlier murders *and* to taking a potshot at you. And since we also have his gun, it's open and shut as far as establishing he did it. Even my snooty and skeptical friends in CPS are prepared to concede that." He paused. "So there! Does knowing all that make you feel relaxed and unstressed, Detective Superintendent?"

Cecilia nodded.

There was a click from the direction of the door. She looked up, as did the others.

The door opened and a plump cheerful nurse entered, wheeling a trolley.

She gave Cecilia a glass of water and with it a selection of variously colored pills from little plastic pots. She checked her temperature and blood pressure. Finally she nodded approvingly and declared that the patient was doing well.

Well, not quite finally.

By way of an encore she announced that the tea trolley should be arriving soon and they would all be welcome to partake. Then she departed.

"I gather," Joseph said slowly, "there are various reasons why killers—even serial killers—may stop killing and lead normal lives for a bit. One is that whoever or whatever's been provoking them to kill disappears, or dies, so they no longer feel the urge to do it. I'm thinking that's what happened with Catesby. My impression is the Major was athletic and sporting and a hit with women, but also self-opinionated and a bit of a bully. A couple of people have said he used to give young Greg a hard time and put him down—and in public, too. So maybe that's what Greg was acting out when he killed those boys— showing that *he* could defend the family honor, too, and be just as tough as Dad."

"Very Freudian," Michael said. "The son wants to replace the father."

"Exactly. But then his dad's *actual* death in the car crash sets him free—free to be a decent fellow."

"Until we start inquiring into the killings and focusing on him and stirring things up all over again," Verity said.

Joseph nodded. "And remember," he said, "he liked Cecilia at first. But then she started pressing him, so she switches in his mind from being a friend to being the enemy—Daddy all over again. *Pace* William Congreve, I'm quite sure it isn't only *woman* scorned that hell doesn't have a fury like!"

Cecilia sighed. "If you're even half right, it makes me wonder whether it wouldn't have been better if we'd left the whole thing alone in the first place. We can't bring back the dead, and we've pushed poor Catesby off his rocker again when he'd actually managed to get his life together."

Glyn Davies stared at her thoughtfully. "Well, after what he did, if any of us has a right to call him 'poor Catesby,' I dare say it's you." He paused. "But then, if we'd left the thing alone, where would have been the justice in that for Jenny Farthing and her family? She'd have gone to her grave with the world thinking her boy was a murderer and a suicide, which he wasn't. God knows, human justice isn't perfect, but that doesn't let us off doing the best we can."

Cecilia nodded. He'd said something in much the same spirit to her after they'd arrested Dennis Reeves, and again to Tom and Headley on the night of the Paris attacks. And now, as then, he had a point.

At which she thought of her dream . . . or vision . . . or near-death experience—or whatever one chose to call it.

And the repair shop.

She looked at Michael. "Well at least we can hope he isn't broken beyond repair."

For a moment Michael looked puzzled, but then he nodded. "So you still remember that! I told you that story ages ago!"

"Trust me! I'm a detective. I remember these things. Anyway, I was sort of . . . reminded of it, recently."

He looked at her quizzically.

She gave him a half smile and a slight shake of her head. She did indeed intend to tell him about her dream . . . or whatever it was. But not here. Not now.

"Later?" she said.

"Absolutely."

"Thank you."

"And so?"

"And so—if nothing is broken beyond repair," she said, "then presumably that would include Gregory Catesby."

"Presumably."

And now that she came to think about it, she actually believed that… most of the time. Although God knows there were days and moments when it wasn't easy.

At which point in her thinking there was a click, and she looked up as the door to her room opened again.

The lady with the tea trolley had arrived.

EPILOGUE

Jenny Farthing died quietly in her sleep on the night of Tuesday, 15th December. She'd been sinking for several days. When Michael visited, he'd find her curled into a little ball, asleep. All he could do was to stand by her bed for a few minutes and pray, and give her a blessing.

But then on the afternoon of the fifteenth he'd found her awake and chirpy. They'd had a nice chat. Yet he knew instinctively that it was also goodbye. He rather thought that she knew it, too. And at the end of it, he gave her the last rites.

"Looks like I'll be with my Tom and our Jimmy just in nice time for Christmas!" she whispered with a twinkle in her eye and a naughty little smile when the rites were done. "'Cept, of course, if the Almighty's got something even better planned for us!"

Jenny's Requiem Eucharist and funeral were on the following Friday morning at St. Mary's Church as Michael had promised her they would be.

He recalled how, the day he met Jenny Farthing, Mrs. Lofton the matron had told him she thought Jenny was lonely. That same evening he'd said to Cecilia that she seemed to have no one. Doubtless it had seemed so at the time, but as it turned out, there was quite a large group gathered in the church that morning to say good-bye to her.

Cecilia came of course, together with Verity and Joseph and everyone on the Serious Crimes Team.

Glyn Davies and Olwen were there. Mrs. Lofton attended, and brought a dozen or so residents from The Blossoms Residential Home—for Jenny Farthing seemed somehow to have made friends with quite a few of them during her short time there, even though for most of it she'd not been well enough to leave her bed. And there was a small group of volunteers that Michael himself had scrambled together from the St. Mary's Sunday choir. They sang the requiem.

Verity read the appointed passage from the Old Testament, Cecilia from the New, and Joseph led the prayers of the people. Michael celebrated and preached. As was his habit at funerals, he spoke mostly not about the deceased but about the Christian hope she shared.

"What does it mean," he asked, "when Paul says, 'Death is swallowed up in victory?' It means, I think, what Mary Magdalen found on the first Easter morning. She stood by an empty tomb, lost in an abyss of failed hopes and her fellow disciples' treacheries and betrayals. And what happened? She was met by a love and forgiveness so vivacious, so powerful, so gloriously alive, she could hardly believe it was the One she had seen die on a cross—until he called her by name. Then when she cried out in joy, 'My teacher!' and tried to embrace him, she was told, 'Not yet!'—an immediate disappointment that was also a promise. 'Not yet! —For I am not yet ascended.' 'Not yet! —For there is more to come.' 'Not yet! —For the joy to which you are destined, the joy you may embrace eternally, is greater even than the joy you see now or could possibly imagine.' This was God's promise to Mary of Magdala, it was God's promise to Jenny Farthing, and it is God's promise to us. Death is swallowed up in victory."

After the funeral there was a reception at The Blossoms arranged by Mrs. Lofton. To Michael's great delight, everyone came. All very English it was, with tiny cucumber sandwiches and small pieces of rich fruitcake and little glasses of Harvey's Bristol Cream sherry.

"She liked her glass of Harvey's Bristol Cream, Jenny did," Mrs. Lofton said to him. "Never more than a glass, mind you! But she did enjoy it."

Did she, indeed! How very Anglican of her! "Here's to Jenny then," he said, raising his glass. "You've certainly given her a good send off!"

"Well so did you, Father! Lovely service it was in the church, I thought."

"Thank you, Mrs. Lofton."

And, he thought, with a secret smile directed toward Jenny Farthing (who in the fuller presence of her God was now doubtless more beautiful than ever—indeed, a bit of all right!), he'd certainly made sure there was plenty of bowing and scraping.

All we go down to the dust; yet even at the grave we make our song: Alleluia, alleluia, alleluia.

All the bowing and scraping in the world.

THE AUTHOR'S NOTES
AND HIS THANKS

Several people have asked me how to pronounce my heroine's name: the key thing is that the "c"s are not pronounced like "s"s but like "ch" in "church." The second syllable is stressed. So her whole name is pronounced, "Checheelya": and actually she is quite fussy about it. I think the other people in my stories either have names that are easy for English speakers to pronounce or else they don't care.

I should acknowledge that ideas for the plot of *The Dogleg Murders* came partly from *Good Work Rewarded*, an early episode (S1, Ep5) in television's *New Tricks* — one of my absolutely favorite British police series: funny, clever, it has everything — and partly from *The Dogleg Murders* episode (S12, Ep1) in the equally splendid *Midsomer Murders*. Of course no one but me is to be blamed for the use I've made of these ideas!

Michael's two stories, the one about the patrol near the German lines and the one about the repair shop, are both real stories, although I have to some extent altered the contexts to fit with my own narrative. The patrol near the German lines is actually a World War I story, and the young officer in nominal command was my friend Leslie Stemp. I got to know him when, then a retired barrister, he was kind enough to allow me to have "digs" in his house in the early 1960s when I was the assistant priest in my first parish, St. Mark's, Reigate, in the county of Surrey. I changed Leslie Stemp's story from World War I to World War II only because I could see no way in which Michael Aarons, who was born in 1971, could possibly have known a World War I veteran when he was in his first parish. The repair shop story came from my friend Charles DuBois, and the shop was actually in New York. But the substance of both stories is otherwise more or less as I remember being told them.

I am aware that Cecilia's dream or vision implies certain views about eternal destiny and the universality of God's saving will. Any who are interested in a more formal statement of those views, or my opinion as to why they are fundamentally the views of Scripture, could look at my *The Resurrection of the Messiah* (Oxford University Press, 2013), especially Appendix H, "The New Testament and the Negative Eschaton: the Possibility of Damnation" (pages 231-33). In particular, some may note that Father Spee (as one might expect of a good sixteenth century Jesuit), in quoting St John's gospel, and in particular quoting John 12:32, follows the *omnia* (presumably translating παντα: "all things") of Jerome's Vulgate rather than the πάντας: "all people," which is the text preferred by most modern translations. In fact the Greek text witnessed to by Jerome is by any standards quite well attested (notably by P⁶⁶ and ℵ* [the uncorrected Sinaiticus]), and the generally asserted reasons for the modern preference are in my view by no means entirely convincing. Again, if anyone is interested in a fuller statement and explanation of that opinion, please see my *Resurrection of the Messiah*, page 358, note 53.

As always I must say "thank you" to my many conversation partners: first and above all to Wendy Bryan, and then among others to Renni Browne, Suzanne Dunstan, Chris Egan, John Gatta, Julia Gatta, Bob Hughes, David Landon, Luann Landon, Rob MacSwain, Sister Madeleine Mary CSM, Susanna Metz, Mary Ann Patterson, Laurie Ramsey, Leslie Richardson, Shannon Roberts, John Solomon, Barbara Stafford, Bill Stafford, and everyone at The Editorial Department. Thank you very much, all of you, for continuing to listen to and answer my questions and in other ways to encourage my pieces of trivia, thereby indulging me in the enormous pleasure I get from writing them.

Christopher Bryan,
Easter, 2016.

ABOUT THE AUTHOR

Photograph by Wendy Bryan

Sometime Woodward Scholar of Wadham College, Oxford, Christopher Bryan is an Anglican priest, novelist, and academic. He and his wife Wendy live in Sewanee, Tennessee, and Exeter, England. His earlier novels are *Siding Star* (Diamond Press, 2012), which was named to Kirkus Reviews Best Books of 2013, *Peacekeeper* (Diamond Press, 2013), *Singularity* (Diamond Press, 2014) and *A Habit of Death* (Diamond Press, 2015). Author and critic Parker Bauer described them in *The Weekly Standard Book Review* as "ideal antidotes to the crypto-farces of Dan Brown."

Christopher Bryan's academic studies include *Listening to the Bible: The Art of Faithful Biblical Interpretation* (Oxford University Press, 2014), *The Resurrection of the Messiah* (Oxford University Press, 2011), the popular *And God Spoke* (Cowley, 2012) (which was among the books chosen as commended reading for the Bishops at the 2008 Lambeth Conference), and *Render to Caesar: Jesus, the Early Church, and the Roman Superpower* (Oxford University Press, 2005).

For more about Christopher Bryan, visit his website at
www.christopherbryanonline.com